God Tied

By: Katherine Coitier

Chapter One

Sometimes life isn't the way you have known it to be or had always seen it. Sometimes it's so far beyond different than anyone could ever thought it could be. That they themselves were far different than what we mere mortals could have thought. Things aren't always what they seem as the saying goes.

For all my life I'd been told how the world really was. That Gods didn't exist except for the big man in the sky. That magic was just in fairy tales. That dreams were only what our minds were using to interrupt things we want or what we've been through. But there are moments in everyone's lives where they realize everything they thought they knew was wrong.

My story begins with a dream...

The fire flickered sweetly in the half domed metal holder that hung just off the golden stone walls. The flames consuming the pieces of small wood and dry reeds that were stacked in the center like a pyramid. The warmth seeped into the room and made it so comfortable for this cold night.

I laid stroking the fur I rested on that was draped over the bedding blankets as they were stacked six high so I was comfortable. The feeling of loneliness thick in my strokes as I have felt for a long time now. The comforting feeling that I usually had never reached me this time. My eyes looking to the empty area next to me wishing for the one warm body that would end my loneliness and longing for them. Someone that should be there already, but they weren't. They had promised, yet still they were not with me.

A sound caught my ear and I rose up hoping it was my love. Hoping that my loneliness had finally come to an end at long last. But when I turned toward the sound, there was no one at all but me. Just as it had been for several months now. Several terribly long months.

The warm golden color of the stone walls glittering with the glow of the fire. But it's warmth couldn't reach me as my heart sank again. My heart just wanting to see him standing there as he had promised.

I laid back down and went back to stroking the fur again. My longing hurting my heart the whole time. Never had he been gone from my side for so long. Never had he broken a promise to me. When he makes a promise, he always keeps it as he was honorable like that. It's what I loved the most about him above all.

A gasp came out as there was a shadow that shrieked across the stones. It caused me to sit up only to have hands grip my wrists and pin me face down on the bed. My heart only picking up because of how quickly the assault happened. Fear not yet hitting me.

"I do this for him." The rough voice proclaimed into my ear in almost a sneer. As if I had done something to this man, but I'd never wrong anyone. My soul would never let me do such a thing. Not in any of my years thus far in this world. A small stitch of fear hit me as I couldn't move him off me.

Before I knew it, there were screams that froze my heart. I thrashed against his hold now, but it was no use. He was somehow stronger than I was. But that was impossible for a mortal. My kind were infinitely stronger than any mortal. All I could do was try to free myself as more screams filled the air. My people needed me.

"Release me this instant." My anger lifted up for a moment as I tried to command him. Anything I could do to save my people, I was going to try. My skin tightening with the need and my rage to seek vengeance.

"Sorry my goddess, but I will not. This is the end for you. I was told how one of you could die and with your death, he'll be free of you."

My breathe caught in my throat. My mind crying out thinking that it was my beloved who was doing this to me. But my soul was shouting that it wasn't as if it knew the truth. He'd never shown any clue that he wished to be raid of me. No hint at all, yet that thought crossed my mind. All he would have had to do was ask and I'd free him, though with a heavy heart the whole time. I'd give him anything and everything he wanted.

But for him to resort to this, I was already dying with the thought. Who else would want me dead if they could arrange it? I was loved by the rest of my kind and by so many within this world.

It didn't take long for another fire to consume my home along with me as I laid unmoving below this suicidal man. I just prayed others were more lucky than I. That they didn't die with me. Glad that all the mortals wouldn't feel everything about being burned alive like I was. Even the man holding me down died before he felt anything like I was feeling, but I was trapped the whole time within my body as the fire burned away every bit of me.

I waited for the moment the last of my body was completely gone. The moment I no longer had a physical form. The whole time feeling every molecule being consumed by the fire. Every atom that made my body up so I could exist in the mortal realm and others. Never have one of my kind ever actually died and now I was the first.

~~~

Something soft draped over my body. Was it my body? I couldn't feel anything that was physical. So I was just a spirit now. Nothing more as I had been.

My ghostly eyes opened and saw Osiris looking down at me where he held my spirit. "I'm sorry. So sorry."

Tears came to my bodiless eyes. My heart breaking yet again. This time more so as my soul cried out in emotional pain. As one of my kind, we could do this as a mortal wouldn't have been able to.

"If he didn't want to be tied to me anymore, he just had to ask." I fell into Osiris as he sat next to me. His arms wrapping around me as no one else could now. He was the God of the dead and only he had the ability to touch a departed soul. Like what I was now.

"My son would have never done this. I know he loves you beyond even this endless life." He tried to comfort me. His words soothing my soul only slightly. My soul was trying to understand why I had to die, but I couldn't understand at all. I thought I had been loved by all and was kind to all. This should never have happened.
~~~

"But now he's free from me and my tie that was between us." I sobbed my heart out as he pulled me infinitely closer.

That's where I stayed for a time. In his arms feeling a father's grief and pain as if he were my own father. For many years I've grown to think of him as a father next to my own.

"Forgive me, but it's time." He whispered into my ear. It was as if he didn't want to do what we had to do next. As if he just wanted to hold onto me and never let go. Not to lose me as a daughter. I didn't want to lose him as a father.

I looked up into his hauntingly white face, just as white as the clouds in the sky or the snow on the ground among the mountains. His red eyes even more red with grief over my passing. "I won't get to see him again, will I?"

Osiris shook his head. "Sorry. He can't be touched even by me now." His heart clearly broken completely by the look on his purest of white faces.

I looked down and let him lift me up. He walked over to the eerie looking water that moved unlike any water in the mortal realm and stepped into it with me in his arms. I had no physical body so I couldn't go to paradise. I had to live again but not as what I was, an immortal goddess. I could be a number of many things including a mortal or a feline. No one ever knows what they'll come back as, not even Osiris himself knows what a person is destined to be when they return.

With the water around us up to our necks, Osiris turned toward me. "Fear not anything. You have my word that I'll watch over you in every life you live." He leaned forward and kissed my forehead before he let go of me. Letting the waters embrace me fully. His kiss still firm on my ghostly forehead.

I closed my eyes and let the water take me. The water crept up the rest of my neck before it slipped up and over my head. It took memory after memory from my mind when I was fully submerged under it's shimmering surface. But those memories of my life swirled around me and never dissolved as it did with mortal memories. My life lingered around me as if it was clinging to remain solid.

Nothing really mattered as my sight faded and I faded deeper within the water. The water pulling me far down into it's ever darkening depths. What I was no longer existed and never will again. I was just like every other mortal now. Just a nameless soul till someone gave me a name.

~*~*~

MEEEP. MEEEP. MEEEP.

My hand came down on my alarm clock as I groaned. Another day and I was exhausted again in the beginning of it. I hated that dream sometimes. It always left me exhausted and as if it took all my energy to see. That it was telling me something that I shouldn't forget.

But what did it really mean?

Every time I had that dream, it felt real, yet was too out there to be real. Gods didn't exist. They were't real. But there was always this part of me that wanted them to be real. To give a reason why things happened even to good people, both good and bad.

I took a deep breathe and smiled to myself. Not even that dream could ruin this moment for me. Finally I had done it. Left the U.S. to go somewhere I have wanted to go for so long. Where I've always dreamt of seeing for myself. Egypt. Specifically to the delta region.

It'd always been my dream to see Bubastis for myself. The temple once dedicated to the Egyptian Goddess Bastet. I don't know why I had been always drawn here, but now I was here. Maybe I'll get some answers as to why I felt so connected to this old place. Why, even as a very small child, I'd find out anything and everything about the area to try and find out why the temple had burned down. I had found nothing at all. Those ruins' secrets fell into the obscurity of history for people to come up with all sorts of theories.

After dressing for the warm weather, I walked down to the dining hall of the hotel I was staying in to get a quick bite to eat before I have to meet the tour going to the ruin. Normally I wouldn't take a tour, but it seemed the easiest way to see the ruins without any trouble on my part. No dealing with cabbies even here in Egypt. Who knows would would happen, and I didn't know how to speak the language here. I knew a few phrases, but not enough to figure out that I was in danger of being kidnapped.

The moment I stepped onto the bus, I went straight to the back. Someplace away from everyone else as most people fill in the front first. I wasn't like everyone else in the least. Especially other Americans. I knew I wasn't the end all be all. I was just me and I didn't even know if that was good enough.

Thankfully I didn't have to wait long for everyone to get on the bus and we were on our way to the ruins. My dream was finally coming true. Though with a bus full of other couples than I was, it was still a dream come true.

The instant we had arrived at the ruins, I broke off from the group and wandered around the ruins privately. It wasn't like I knew the ruins, but those kind of groups were just not my ideal way to see such a beautiful sight such as this. I preferred the quiet and peaceful wandering to take in the ruins at my own pace. I did however snatch one of the maps of the ruins that the group provided so I could find my way around with very little problem.

Normally I'm cautious when I start feeling curious, but there are times my curiosity just gets the better of me. This is one of the latter times as my eyes landed on some activity on the far side of the ruins. There seemed to be something going on at that part with the area roped off. I walked up to the area where there were a number of people milling around and discussing something.

"Excuse me." I said tapping lightly on a guy's shoulder that was leaning against a pole that held a rope that went around the sight. Signs that said that this area of the ruins was off limits to unauthorized personnel. A rope intended to keep onlookers like myself out of the area but giving up the ability to peep into the activity from afar. I only knew that as there was English along with other languages on the signs.

The gentleman turned around toward me. The moment he did, his eyes looked me over and he grinned as if he like what he saw. "Yes Miss?" He purred as he leaned his hip against the pole lightly again. It shifted a little under his weight. I'm not saying he's heavy, just that it really wasn't designed for people to lean on.

"What are they doing?" My curiosity giving voice as I looked around him for a heartbeat at the area. Then my eyes went back up to his that remained on me.

He raised an eyebrow. A slight smirk to his lips as he offered an amused explanation. "We are looking for a lost room to this once beautiful temple for one of the most beloved Gods in ancient Egyptian history." There was even humor in his voice as he said we. As if there was some kind of joke hidden within his words and was going on in his mind.

I frowned up at him. "Why are you looking for this room?" Yet again my curiosity slipping out before I could stop it. I was berating myself internally for just saying whatever was passing through my mind.

"I've long theorized that this room we are looking for still contains treasure untouched since the fire that destroyed this temple. Those of us in the archeological community hope that it will help us understand more of this once great temple." He lifted the rope. "Do you want to watch?"

I looked to the rope and then back at him. Unsure yet so curious at the same time. I wanted to cross the line and join in but I knew it was wrong to do that as I wasn't an authorized person to be on that side of the rope. He didn't know me, yet he's right there holding the rope up for me to cross.

"I don't think I'm allowed to cross the line. There's no real reason why I need to be with you all."

He leaned closer to me. "To tell you the truth, not many people here really need to be here." He shrugged. "If anyone asks, you're my assistant from America."

I tilted my head a little at him. "Who are you?"

He chuckled before he stuck his hand out. "Siris Denton, Professor of Archeology for NYU. My area of specialty is in Egyptian history."

I shook his hand timidly. "Bea Skylar."

"A pleasure to meet you." He said as he pulled me across the line effortlessly making me gasp at him. "Let's join the fun as we fully figure out where we will start our search."

All I could do was trail sightly behind him nervously as he walked up to the ones holding a set of what looked like some building plans for the ruins. My eyes wandered around as he conversed with several people as they were continuing their debate of certain spots. Some places next to the stone wall next to us and others away from it.

This part of the ruins seem to be the least touched by anything but the weather and time. The least amount of destroyed ruins. As if something had been protecting this spot most of all.

I shyly moved to a wall that seemed weather worn but untouched none-the-less like everything else. Raising my hand, I touched the wall and closed my eyes. A feeling of being taken back in time swept over me. Just to feel a piece of Bubastis. A piece of history that I felt a kinship to for no reason that I could say. Just a feeling of coming home for the first time in a very long time.

"What do you see when you feel the stone?" I smiled as Siris whispered softly into my ear. He was so close to me, but he wasn't touching me where he stood behind me. As if a touch would break the spell that had washed over me. He sounded just as curious as I felt.

Images drifted into my mind and they just flowed out of my mouth unhindered. "Golden stones catching the light from lamps hanging from the walls. People walking down the hall as they always did. Cats everywhere as they should be."

"What else?" He whispered even more softly into my ear holding another sound within it too. It was like he feared speaking any louder than that or else it would dispel the vision and it would be lost forever. I would have to thank him later as I found myself caught in the images dancing around behind my eyelids. Images I embraced wholeheartedly as if I needed them with all my heart and soul.

I turned my head and unconsciously started to walk as if I was walking down the hall I saw in my mind. I stopped in front of a doorway and frowned with eyes still closed. My hand was touching stone where there shouldn't be if my mind was right. Pushing against the stone, it moved and I gasped as my eyes snapped open.

My body suddenly found itself falling. People were shouting as the light faded to dark and thick shadows. The once solid floor beneath my feet was no longer holding me up. I saw Siris lung for me but his hand just missed mine by a mere breath. He was shouting my name and it echoed off the dark, blackened walls. The sun fading as I fell into utter and terrifying darkness that made my panic rise beyond just falling. I feared the dark.

My breath was taken from me was I hit the bottom. The world went dark as I felt my head hit the stone floor heavily. Vaguely I saw someone lean over me as my vision was drifting away. I heard a voice, but it faded with everything else into the black abyss that was unconsciousness.

~~~

I felt a searing pain in my wrist when I came back around for a moment. I felt dizzy as I shifted my head to the side. The pain in my head was overruling the one that I now started to feel in my wrist. A hiss came out, but I couldn't move. I was weak and the world wouldn't stop spinning around me.

"Be still. I'm almost done." A deep smooth voice said as more burning came. I had never felt anything like what was being done to my wrist before which means I didn't understand what could be happening. I had no idea what that voice was doing to me. For the moment, I really didn't care either. Not with how my head hurt so bad.

I struggled to open my eyes and succeeded for a second. What I saw was beyond strange, beyond words. The man next to me holding my wrist wasn't a real man. He had the body of a man, but the head of a hawk. His beady golden eyes shifted to mine before they flicked back down to my wrist. Something was in his free hand and it hurt when it touched me like pins.

My eyes rolled back in my head as I passed out from sheer pain. All I could feel was pain which meant I wasn't fully gone from the world. But I wasn't fully aware either, but say for pain. Slowly even that left me to nothing. There was just nothing.

~~~

My eyes scrunched as a light seemed to blind me through my closed eyes. "Bea!" I groaned hearing my name. "Thank the stars above." The voice now came from next to me. Weird sounds were also coming to my ears too as I was slowly and painfully waking up more. "She's alive!" I winced at the sound of a shout from next to me even if it wasn't downward toward me.

I opened my eyes and saw a blurry form of a man. I couldn't make out who it was, but I knew him from somewhere. My mind was just not processing who it was. I tried. The pain in my head was preventing any recollection to hit me so I could remember anything let alone placing a name to a face.

He turned down to look at me and stroked my hair gently. Almost in a caring kind of way. "We'll get you out of here in a moment Bea. Just don't fall back asleep again. Stay with me."

I raised my hand and he instantly took it. Then he was turning it over. "Where did you get this?" My eyes traveled to my wrist to see the hazy dark lines. There was something there, but I couldn't make it out. "You like ancient egypt so much that you got a tattoo with some of the oldest hieroglyphics." He looked closer almost studying it.

My eyes started to flutter close again and his head snapped back to my face. "Come on. Just a little longer Bea. They're coming down now to get you out." But I couldn't stop myself from slipping away even with him protesting. Panic thick in his words as he shouted my name trying desperately to keep me from passing out again.

~~~

Beep. Beep. Drip. Drip.

I whimpered against those awful sounds. I hated them because that meant that I was in the hospital. I never had a good experience in the hospital. My mother died in one after she lost her battle with cancer. My dad showing up, but saying he couldn't take me in. That he wasn't going to claim me after my mom died because he didn't believe I was his. I had no one at all after that. Even the man my mother had been married to at the time of her death turned away from me.

A hand took mine and gave me a light squeeze. "You're alright now. Just take it easy." I opened my eyes to see Siris staring down at me. I recognized him this time as my head didn't hurt nearly as much. His eyes showing sadness and I knew what it was about, me. "Will you
~~~

forgive me for pulling you across the line?" Yep, I was right. He felt guilty about what happened.

I gave him a small smile. "Not your fault." My voice was cracky.

He shook his head. "You wouldn't have gotten hurt if I hadn't." Something else flashed across his eyes, but it was so fast that it could have been mistaken hat it happened in the first place. "Forgive me." He pleaded again as if I hadn't already had.

I slowly shook my head. "Sometimes things happen for a reason."

He chuckled lightly shaking his head now. "You should be one of my students. I bet you could teach them a thing or two." He smiled down to me.

I grimaced. "I never got the chance to go to college. Still can't. Coming here was once in a lifetime opportunity. I saved up so I could see Bubastis just once." I looked up at the ceiling. "I may never be able to come back." I just had always wanted to see it even if it was once. Once was enough.

He frowned. "As an apology, I'll pay for you to come back with all expenses included. Just say the word whenever and you can come back." He placed his hand in mine again giving me a squeeze. "Any time." He said it as if it was the most important promise in all the world.

I frowned at him as he started to grin thinking of how to make this up to me. I shook my head and winced. "I can't let you do that."

He sat up straighter. "But I insist."

I laughed just to groan at the pain in my head. I lifted my hand to place on my forehead just to frown at my wrist now. I looked over at Siris showing him my wrist and what was on it. "What happened?"

He frowned at me. "You didn't get that done?" I shook my head. He looked confused as he took out his phone scrolling for something on it. "When I found you at the bottom of the shaft, you had a fresh tattoo on your wrist. I assumed you had it done here in town before you showed at the ruins." He showed me a picture. "The odd thing is, the tattoo is almost like a brand tying you to the Egyptian God Horus. A very old spell from what I could find."

I looked at the picture on his phone and saw my wrist. Inked in a deep blood red were hieroglyphics like a pendant. "How did I get it? I hate needles and never would have gotten a tattoo."

"If you didn't have it before you fell, than somehow it showed up while you were down in the shaft all alone." He tapped his chin. "But how? You were down there for a good half an hour before we were able to get the equipment over the hole and for me to propel down to you."

I looked at my wrist. "What could it mean?"

"Some of the workers were saying you've been touched by the Gods. Half believe it's a good thing and that you're protected by a God. The others, not so much. They fear you've been cursed by one. Horus to be exact."

"What does it mean to be tied to Horus?"

Siris shrugged. "I'm still looking into it." He titled his head to the side. "Do you know the different Gods in Egyptian mythology?" It sounded like he was the curious one now as he wandered about what I knew.

I nodded. "But my head hurts. Please refresh my bruised mind."

He smirked. "Horus was the God that had the head of a hawk. He was the God protector of the pharaoh. Son to Osiris and Isis."

I frowned as an image of someone with the face of a hawk looked into my eyes. "I still don't understand." I closed my eyes as more confusion swept over me.

His hand stroke my hair. "You just need to rest. You had a bit of a concussion when you hit the shaft floor. All this talking must not be helping you. Are you in any pain?"

"A little." My voice was sound soft and light as I was getting tired more. Between closing my eyes and his hand moving over my hair had me drifting away little by little. I didn't want to admit it, but his touch was soothing my soul partially.

"That's it. Just rest. I'll look after you." The light shifted just a bit and his skin faded to white for just a hair of a moment. My dream and life merged together oddly.

"Thank you Osiris..."

Chapter Two

"Here, let me get it for you." I frowned at Siris as he leaned over to retrieve my lone suit case off the carousel in the airport's baggage claim. He had insisted on seeing that I got home safely. He hasn't even let me pay for anything at all. Even for my hotel bill which he paid for before I was down to the front desk to do so myself.

When he straightened up, he shook his head at me, then he tapped my nose as if he were my best friend or brother. As if we have known each other our entire lives. "Stop frowning. Like I said, I wish to make sure nothing else happens to you."

I shook my head at him as he took my hand. Then I blushed looking down at his hand. A guy never really held my hand like this before, or any way for that matter. There had never been a guy who liked me enough to treat me sweetly or kindly. I'm not saying I've never been kissed, but still...they never saw me like that. I was the 'sister' and never the 'girlfriend' type of girl to them.

He looked back at me and raised an eyebrow. "You're blushing." He stated sounding very amused by it.

I looked down blushing just a bit more now that he saw that I was. "Guys don't hold my hand." I bit back the word ever so he didn't know that part of my sad little life.

He chuckled. "They are missing something wonderful then." He shrugged. "Their loss." He said as he raised his other hand after setting down my suitcase and hailed a cab outside of the airport. I winced at the high pitched whistle he squealed for the cab to get their attention. It was affective, yet I was still battling a headache from the fall.

One of the cabbies was quicker than I had ever seen to get to us in a matter of a second. The cabbie was even polite enough to get our bags that were next to Siris. Siris had the passenger door open for me making me blush a little more at how much he was a gentleman toward me. Another thing I wasn't used to.

As the door closed, my heart raced when I caught a glimpse of a big bulky guy with the head of a hawk amongst the crowd shifting this way and that outside the airport doors. Horus. One second he was there looking at me, then he was just gone when the crowd covered him up for a split second. I searched for another second for him before Siris was in the back of the cab with me.

I must be a bit jumpy since I woke up from the hospital. I've been seeing him everywhere I turn. My imagination going wild since I fell. He would always only appear briefly. Always just a glimpse. And I'm always the only one to see him. He just looks at me as if I was someone he desired. No one else seems to see him at all like he didn't exist. It was possible he didn't except in my mind.

Looking down at my wrist, I rub it gently. It was still sore and still a bit fresh. My unexpected tattoo was still dressed with some bandages as the docs said they felt that would be best when traveling back. I've made sure to do as they requested for its care. No need to get an infection with my first ever tattoo that I didn't ask for.

When I looked up, we were pulling to the curb in front of my apartment. Siris was out in a flash. I was lucky to get my door open before he was there helping me out. Then he was right there paying for the taxi while I snuck my suitcase from his side.

Siris laughed as he turned around lifting his bag and draping it over his shoulder. "You are as silent as a cat."

I shrugged. "You want to come up and relax for a bit. I know your flight is tomorrow. You could stay in my apartment for the night."

He smiled. "Thanks, but I don't wish to impose on you."

"You paid for my hospital stay, my hotel, and feel guilty for me falling down into a shaft that revealed the room you were searching for. The least I can do is let you stay the night in my sad excuse of an apartment." I said as I opened my door to my place. "Oh... I hope you don't mind cats." I told him as my cats started to show up. One by one, they came in through the window.

They weren't all my cats either. Just strays that came and went as they wished. I have only two cats that stay with me permanently. They rarely leave my place even just to chase a bird or squirrel. Those two were my cats. My babies. The ones that curled up with me at night and slept in my arms purring softly.

Siris laughed as most of my cats detour to him and were sniffing all over him. Soon he's knocked down and they became a blanket on top of him. His laughs were booming around the whole apartment. Filling the place for the first with true joy.

But it wasn't getting anywhere near me. I felt everything closing in on me. The air thickened as I tried to breathe. My wrist burned a little. I gripped the back of my couch before the sounds quieted and I felt Siris lifting me up into his arms. "Just breathe through it. You're still recovering and had been on a long flight back."

He made a soft clicking noise as I felt him laying me down on my bed. I felt two familiar soft fur bodies curl up with me and I hugged them to me nuzzling softly at their heads. Purrs greeted me to my joy.

"Just rest some. Take a nap. You'll feel better after." I nodded to him and settled completely onto my bed. I felt a few more little bodies curl around me. I smiled lightly at the feeling as I drifted off to sleep.

~*~*~

"Love." The adoring voice made me giggle softly as I turned over and opened my eyes to a wonderful sight.

Laying next to me was the most glorious man I ever knew existed. His dark reddish brown hair fell in soft waves down his shoulder and to the soft bedding beneath us. His deep golden eyes looking right into mine. His smile warmed my heart and ageless soul. The feeling of everything being so perfect was what I felt around him, and was something I never wanted to ever end.

He raised a hand up and stroked my cheekbone with the back of his fingers before moving to bury his hand into my hair. He pulled me forward toward him, and kissed me long and slowly, taking his time. His kiss went far deeper than anything ever could. To a place that was just his forever.

We broke apart laughing as we were splashed by some water from the Nile around us and beneath us. Our boat gliding delicately across the Nile. I looked out and smiled at the water and shore. My hand dipped into the water as our ship sailed along gracefully. The sky was spread wide and a deep blue that contrasted the warm sand below it.

"I wish we could stay like this forever. For there to be no wars, no fighting so you could always be with me."

He shifted us and hovered over me. His hair cascading and grazing the sides of my face as he nodded his head. "I wish such a thing too. But the mortals are ever violent and warring. I'm needed next to the pharaoh during battle. It is my duty."

I sighed. "Than I shall enjoy you as long as I can."

He smirked as he leaned down. "As I will you for every blissful second." His lips came to mine with desire and intent. I gave in completely wanting what he was giving me. Cherishing it with all my soul.

~*~*~

I woke and laid on my bed for a moment longer. Just taking in being home. Sadness started washing over me from my dream. He was sweet and so seductive like always. That had not been the first time I had dreamed of him. My heart wished for someone like that for my own. Wanting love like that. Not just in a dream, but in real life.

Taking a deep breathe, I'm greeted with a delicious smell. A sweet and tangy type of scent. My mouth was watering at the smell. I'm wondering if it was what really woke me up from my dream or me.

"I was just coming to wake you."

I rose up from my bed to see Siris leaning against my doorframe to my room. The way he was seemed like something someone would do after knowing someone a long time. As if it were normal for him to be in my apartment.

I wiped the rest of the sleep that lingered in my eyes. "I think whatever that delicious smell is woke me."

He laughed. "So I did manage to wake you gently." He came over and stretched out a hand to me. "I made dinner for us. Since you have been so kind as to offer me to stay with you for the night, I thought I'd make dinner for us." He grabbed my hand and helped me up from my bed. My body feeling weightless for a second with his aid.

I looked to my hand that was once again in his. It felt so familiar yet not romantic just like before. I felt protected and safe as if he were a brother or my best friend. Someone I had known for a long time though we just met.

He took me to my small dining table that was more a dinette set than a dining table. There rested different bowls and plates of food. Oddly enough, none of the cats were on the table like they usually were. I was so used to them eating some of my food before I got the chance to begin. I never minded one bit. This was just different from what I was used to.

I blushed when he pulled a chair out for me being the gentleman again. "For you my lady." His voice sounding like an English lord as he gestured for me to sit. A soft giggle was bubbling inside my chest at that, but I dared not let it out.

I shyly sat down. "Thank you." I watched him walk around the table and take his seat across from me. "You didn't have to do this. We could have just ordered something. I know several great places that deliver."

He shook his head as he moved his napkin to his lap. "Nonsense. I rarely order out when in the US." He shrugged as he spooned some rice onto my plate before he did the same for his own plate. "Food in the US always didn't taste right to me."

I lifted a lid to a plate near me and found flaky delicious fish filets that were seared to perfection. "I felt the same, but I didn't have fish in my fridge."

He chuckled as he added some veggies to my plate. "I went out to the store near by. I also stocked your cupboard for you."

I shook my head at him. "You're doing too much for me."

He shook his head right back at me. "You are back and were in need of some food." He peeled off a small flake of the fish on his plate and fed it to a close by cat that was rubbing his leg. "I also got them some fresh fish for treats. They already had one filet as I was cooking." He reached down and stroked the little cat that he just fed. "This one didn't get much." The cute tabby was purring up a storm.

I frowned at the little one. "You're too good to us all."

He shook his head again. "I love cats."

I smiled. "I do too."

We fell into a silence as we ate the dinner he created. The meal he made was beyond anything I ever had in all my life outside of a restaurant. Sweet yet hearty. I felt as if I was being taken back to another time. Taken to a place long forgotten. A place taken from me at some point. But I can't recall where or when. All I could do was enjoy what Siris created for us to eat.

My mom had never been around to even cook a meal. She was always off with some guy having the time of her life. She couldn't care less what had happened to me. So there were no home cooked meals growing up unless I made something for myself.

My dad? I had no clue who he was for most of my life. Just some guy my mom was foolish enough with to create me. He may have never cared that I existed. Apparently she found out she was carrying me after she left him and went back to her husband. Even when my mom died and my real father came to the funeral, he saw me then turned and left without ever wanting to see me again as if there was something terrible about me being his daughter. He denied being my father entirely.

At the end of the meal, Siris wiped his mouth and smiled placing the napkin on the table next to his plate. He then placed his elbows on the edge of the table with his hands threaded together where he rested his chin. He was looking at me curiously.

"Tell me Bea. What do you do?"

I frowned. "Nothing really. I just do what my boss needs me to do. You could call me an assistant, but I don't get paid enough for that title." I grimaced. "Not even by half." Yeah, I just barely get paid little more than minimum wage.

He matched my frown. "Than come work for me. I can have an apartment ready and anything else you might need for you to come to New York." He smirked. "You'd get to visit all over the world if you work for me."

I twisted my water glass on the table with my uninjured hand. The offer sounding very tempting, but I knew my current boss all too well.

"That would be nice, but you don't know that much about me. I could mess up terribly and then where would I be? Jobless and owing you so much for your kindness."

He shook his head. "I doubt you would mess up at all. I'd be there with you in the beginning helping you adjust and learn anything you need to learn. At the moment I have no assistant and have been looking for one."

I sighed. "I just don't know."

He reached over and rested his hand on mine. "Take some time to think about it. There is no rush in deciding. The offer is open for whenever you decide to accept. Just know that you have options."

I gave his hand a little squeeze after I twisted my palm upward. "Thank you." Maybe in time he'll see what everyone seems to see, I'm not worth it.

"Now come on. There has to be something on that will entertain us." He pulled me up from the table which became bombarded by cats after we got up. "They've been waiting till we got up."

I giggled. "My sweet vacuum cleaners."

He laughed as I sat down on one side of the couch letting him have the remote. He tried handing it to me but I insisted he have it as he was my guest. He'd just laugh and pull me to his side letting me lean against him. My heart skipping a beat that we were cuddling together on the couch.

In the end, I fell back to sleep watching Cleopatra with Siris. We had fun talking about Egypt as we did. Talking about anything and everything about the land we just came back from. By the time it was halfway through, we were just watching the movie quietly. All conversation died down comfortably.

I whimpered lightly when I was lifted up. "Just taking you to bed." I heard Siris whisper into my ear. His voice took on a different sound. Something so...godly in a way that had the feeling of authority. But there was also something else to it. Something I couldn't place my finger on but wished I'd heard most of my life.

There was a clicking sound from him again as he set me down on my bed. His hand stroked my hair and I felt him kiss my forehead. "I hope he takes very good care of you when I'm gone. If ever you need me..." He stroked my hair. "Just call me. Think of me and I'll be by your side." He whispered into my hair before there was another kiss.

I heard the faint sound of footsteps before the soft click of my door closing. I relaxed into sleep again in my bed. I knew things were changing. I could feel the change deep within my bones. Even my wrist burned telling me it already had started.

Chapter Three

I woke to the sun shining happily in through my window. It's rays warming where they rested against my body. It was something I always enjoyed when I didn't have to wake up before sunrise to go to work.

Rolling over to my other side, I felt a piece of paper crunch under my shoulder. I knew it was out of place as it wasn't there when I went to sleep. Lifting it, I saw my name scrawled across it in a handwriting I didn't recognize.

Bea,

By the time you read this, I will be on my way back to New York. I thank you for your hospitality and the pleasure of meeting all your wonderful cats. They were quite entertaining with their curiosity over me.

Please take your time to consider my offer to become my assistant. Even in the short amount of time knowing you, I'm convinced that we would work well together. You are smart and quick. To top it off, you know my field maybe better than my students do. I feel you would thrive better by my side than where you are now. Let me help you know a better life.

Take whatever time you need. If you need a few years, than so be it. I just want to keep our contact open and maybe lure you to Egypt again in hope to persuade you.

I hope you enjoy the rest of your week off though you aren't in Egypt any longer. Again I'm sorry for ending your trip too soon. I know your cats love having you back. At least you won't have to go into work for a time.

Your newest annoying friend,
Siris Denton

P.S. If you ever need me, contact me. Even if it is to talk about nothing at all. I want us to be good friends.

At the bottom of the letter, Siris gave me his contact information. Anything I could use to talk to him if I wanted. Email. Cell. Even house and office numbers.

I groaned as my phone rang after I set the letter aside. There weren't too many people who actually called me at all. "Hello." I greeted the caller a little groggily. All I wanted to do was curl back up under my covers and hide from the world a little longer.

"So it's true! You returned early." I groaned out not wanting to hear his voice at all. That sneering and hate filled voice.

"Only because I got hurt. I was told it'd be best to return home in order to recover properly." Especially how I was panicking a little while in the hospital. The doctors didn't want me to have the added stress they noticed they were adding to me. I was to have a stress-free environment, yet hearing my boss' voice wasn't so stress-free at all.

"Well you can recover in the office."

I sat up quickly with my eyes wide and my jaw dropped down to my covers. He couldn't be serious! "You can't do that. I am still on holiday."

"I can and I have. I expect you in the office in an hour." I pulled my phone away from my ear when I heard the sharp click of him hanging up on me. He ended the call not giving me any choice in the matter.

That was how my boss treated me. Like his own personal slave. I rarely get time off. He tries everything to keep me in the office past working hours and doesn't even pay me the proper overtime that I deserve. He makes my life hell most of the time.

I looked to my wrist as it stung a little. "I wish I really did have my own personal god."

"All you have to do is ask."

I yelped and covered my mouth staring at a very broad shouldered, deep tan skinned, hawk face guy at the end of my bed. His amber golden eyes looking right at me as they have for days now. He was also wearing the old Egyptian style loincloth resembling a kilt from the old kingdom that barely hit his knees emphasizing the golden laced sandals that were wrapped around his ankles.

He tilted his head to the side. His feathers shifting with his movements. "You look confused." He started to walk around the bed and I scrambled off the other side which made him stop just passed the foot of the bed. "You need not be afraid of me. We are tied to each other."

I glared at him shoving my wrist toward him. The image of what he put on it still looking red and sore. "I didn't ask for this. You force your brand on me."

His eyes went to the tattoo and he reached out placing his whole hand around it. His fingers wrapping fully around my wrist completely while his palm increased the heat of that sensitive area. "I meant no harm to you." I gasped as my skin started tingling instead of burn. The tingles spread out from the area and down my body to my toes.

He gently pulled me forward causing me to bend over the bed slightly. His other hand catching my cheek keeping me from falling all the way onto the bed. The bed being the only thing separating us from each other.

His touch was doing many things to me. My heart raced as his thumb rubbed my lips. I was also breathing heavy. His eyes trapping mine. "You are the first I have seen for over three thousand years. You're the one fate gave to me." He whispered as his eyes watched his thumb.

I shook myself from the haze he caused in me. I tugged my wrist away and he let go instantly. His other hand falling away too. He was letting me go. Instantly I'm rubbing my wrist only to realize it didn't hurt anymore. "Thank you."

I looked up at him and he was watching me. Almost studying me. "I caused the pain, I should have come sooner to take it away."

Looking over at my alarm clock, I groaned. "I really don't have time for this." I huffed as I marched over to my dresser and pulled out my quickest outfit from my drawers. "Thank you for taking the pain away, but I need to get ready for work that I shouldn't be forced to do today."

He grabbed my arm gently and spun me around when I tried to rush past him. "I don't understand. You shall not be forced to do anything at all."

I sighed tugging my arm from him. "The world isn't the same simple place it once was." I told him as I turned away and slipped into my bathroom. “People are made to do many things they don’t want to in order to survive.” I closed the door leaving me alone.

The door to the bathroom opened and closed in the middle of my shower. I stuck my head out to see him standing with his back to me. "Do you mind? I'm taking a shower." I threw the curtain closed again turning my back on him.

"Forgive me. I couldn't stay out there any longer."

"Bored?"

He chuckled. "Yes." I heard him start to mess with a few things. "I only know a few things about the world as it is now." There was a sigh. "I was supposed to know all you know, but something went wrong. I need your help to know this new kind of world."

"Why didn't you get my knowledge if you were supposed to?"

There was a groan. "Something about you is different. Like you're not a normal mortal."

I sighed turning the water off. "There's nothing special about me." My voice sounding so very sad. That was drilled into me by so many as I grew up. Classmates chanted it every chance they got. My boss repeats it just to keep me down.

I pulled a towel into the shower stall and wrapped myself in it. "Please leave for a moment while I dress."

"I'll always be close to you. I fear we need time to figure things out and I see you don't have the time now." I heard the curtain move and then his fingers graced my arm. "If you need anything of me, grace your wrist. I'll feel it as if you touched me and I'll come to you instantly."

His hand just started to wisp away. Turning to see him, I found he was fully gone. I was left completely alone now, but I knew I wasn't ever going to be fully alone. He would always be near. That I knew deep down even as I look to the tattoo he placed on my wrist.

I left without breakfast and hailed a cab. Opening my purse just to find a small wrapped sandwich which was warm and a small note written on top. "Morning meal is important. Keeps a mortal strong." The symbol of a bird at the bottom told me it was from Horus.

Eating the sandwich, I swallowed the moan that so desperately wanted to get out. He was good just like Siris had been last night. The taste taking me back to another time too. Both seemingly able to invoke such a powerful of a recollection that I shouldn't have. That didn't make any sense with my life either, but I couldn’t think about it right now.

I arrived five minutes early to the office. My boss stood with his arms folded and he was scowling at me. Nothing out of the ordinary about that either. "You're late!"

Typical. "But sir. You called less than an hour ago." I said timidly.

He grabbed my arm roughly, glaring darkly at me. "You dare backtalk to me." He shoved me down onto my desk. My hands falling to the surface so I didn’t topple over. "Get my coffee before I lose my temper and you don't want me to lose my temper." He matched to his office and slammed the door.

Looking around, I noticed everyone else wasn't in. I didn't like this knowledge. Alone with Seth Dath, my boss. My evil and abusive boss that has left bruises before. Being alone with him could not be good. I've tried to make complaints and even tried to find another job, but he found a way to make everyone turn against me. Like I said before, he makes my life hell with no chance for escape.

For most of the day, I just had to try and keep up with the rants my boss would go on and the demands he issued. Lunch was barely existent. If it wasn't for a new sandwich showing up magically in my desk drawer, I wouldn't have been able to eat. But even that didn't last long as my boss stormed out and snatched the sandwich from my hand throwing it into the trash saying that I didn't have time to waste on eating anything.

The second I got home, my phone rang as my front door clicked shut. "Please tell me this isn't my boss." Yeah, not a good way to greet anyone on the other end. I was just too exhausted to care at the moment.

There was a booming laugh on the other end. "Not unless you agreed to come up here and work for me."

"Oh thank god!" I groaned out loudly.

"I was just calling to see how your day went."

"Not good at all." I whimpered/whined holding back the sob as a tear fell. Being too tired to even wipe it away.

"What happened?" He said sounding very sympathetic.

I sighed laying down on my sofa with my legs hanging over the armrest. My whole body felt worn and tired. "My jerk of a boss found out I was back ahead of schedule and declared that I had to work. That my vacation was over."

"Than come work for me. I'd never do that to you, ever!" His voice was fierce but gentle toward me. His voice telling me that he was pissed at my boss but trying to convince me. Like he was wanting only what was best for me.

"I still don't know. We barely know each other. And above all that, I need my job to pay my bills. If he found out you are looking to hire me, he'll do everything in his power to make it so you didn't want me. That's his sick little game to keep me under his thumb."

"Than come out here now. Send in your resignation and hop on the first flight out here with your two cats. I can have you on a flight in the morning. He won't know what hit him."

I sighed thinking that it was too simple, there had to be a flaw in that plan. "Where would I live? How will I buy groceries?" How will I explain the Egyptian God hanging around me? That would certainly raise Siris' eyebrows.

I gasped as I felt a hand on my knee. Speaking of the God himself. Horus had a frown on his face. I looked to my wrist and realized I just rubbed it. Wow. Talk about a God on demand.

His hand slid down to my shoes and he took them off for me one by one. I sighed with each of them coming off before I realized that Siris was still on the phone. "Hey Siris, I'll talk to you later, okay?"

"Yeah sure. But please think about my offer. I'll pay for everything, just say yes. It'll be my job to see that you're taken care of if you would agree to it."

"I'll think about it. Just give me some time to go over everything in my head. This would be a huge step and I don't know if I'm comfortable with it."

"Think about it and rest well." He told me before he hung up.

I moaned fully now that I was off the phone as Horus was knelt down next to the sofa massaging my feet. "Why are you doing that?" I asked not caring that I voiced my curiosity without hesitation.

He frowned the best he could with a hawk's face. His eyes turning down was what really told me he was sad because of my question. "You are exhausted and sore." He shook his head as his eyes flared with anger. "He treats you terribly. Like a slave which you are not." He looked deep into my eyes. "Give me permission to smit him for you."

I frowned at him. "You can't do that."

"Why not?"

I closed my eyes as I started to feel dizzy. "Please. I just need to relax and not worry about anything right now."

His hand came to my hair and he started to stroke the length of it almost adoringly. "Just say the word. Tell me you wish better and he will be taken care of by my hands." His words were soft as if I was his goddess instead of him being the god.

Turning my head toward him, I looked at him with my frown still on my face. "He's done nothing to be killed for." Except for being a jerk. And evil.

I tilted my head to the side. "Do you always have a hawk head?" The words just came tumbling out.

He chuckled as he shook his head. As he shook, his face shifted and changed. His feathers gave way to luscious black hair. His beak compressed and formed a nose and lips. His eyes thinned out to human eyes.

A gasp slipped my lips and I rose up seeing him. "It's you." My voice trembled in shock. "But how?"

He looked at me confused. "None have known my human face for many a millennia." He took a step to me and I rounded the back of the sofa placing it between us. His eyes turning pained. "I thought we were passed this."

"You just took on the form of the man from my dreams, didn't you? You used his image from my mind."

He tilted that handsome head of his that has sent my heart fluttering more than once throughout my whole life. "That cannot be. As

I've stated before, the knowledge I should have gain when tying you to me, I never received. There's something wrong with our connection. I have only received knowledge that is purely that, knowledge. Anything that's tied to a memory is blocked from me."

I frowned moving again as he took a step toward me. "But..." I placed a hand on my forehead as I felt dizzy. "I don't understand."

He gripped my arms and guided me back to the couch. He helped lay me back down across the length of it. "You are still unwell. Rest and I'll take care of you."

My hand gripped his arm as he started to get up. "Something's wrong with... me..." Everything went dark as he cupped my face. He was shouting, but I couldn't hear anything.

~*~*~

The sky blazed in reds and golds. I stood leaning against a column with my shoulder against it. A happy smile on my face. My life felt even more perfect now than ever before.

Today had been perfect. The tying ceremony was beyond beautiful no matter that it was private for the actual ceremony. My father wasn't too keen that I was tying myself to Horus, but he couldn't deny how much I was in love. Osiris looked happy and he's always been like a father to me more than my own.

A hand slipped onto the side of my face and turned it to my beloved Horus. His own lips lifting a bit with happiness and love for me. "Was today how you envisioned for us?" He pulled me close.

"I could have never thought of a more perfect day to be tied to you."

He smiled and his golden eyes looked at me with a love beyond the heavens or the seas. "Even on the gloomiest of days, today would have been perfect to me."

I smiled. "As it would have been for me. Just to be with you and to be called yours is all I want. All I will ever need."

A giggle slipped out of my lips as Horus threw me into his arms. "Then shall I show you what I've dreamt to do to you for several centuries. From the moment I saw you."

He laid me down on my bed that had been prepared for the two of us. His hand went to the back of my head as his lips adored mine with an intensity that made my toes curl. Every bit of his love flowed through our kiss and I did the same.

Chapter Four

Beep.

Beep.

My head was killing me. My body wouldn't move. It felt like a hundred pound weights were tied to my limbs to hold them down. No matter how much I tried, I wasn't able to do anything. I couldn't moved even a millimeter. Not even to open my eyes.

A hand slipped into mine as another stroked my hair. "Bea. Tell me you're coming around now." I heard Siris' voice. But that didn't make any sense, he was in New York.

Another hand took my free hand. My tattoo tingling as his fingers brushed against it softly. My body feeling lighter, better. "I feel you. Just relax. Wake when you're ready." Horus' voice whispering down to me. His other hand gracing my cheek delicately.

I took in several deep breathes. My head shifting to the side. When my eyes finally opened slightly, I smiled as a tear left my eye. "Horus." I whispered to the blurry man.

The man I was smiling at chuckled. "Sorry Bea. Wrong guy." He smiled and I could make him out a little more now.

"Siris?"

He nodded. "I'm right here." His hand pet my hair some more. "After our phone conversation, I got on the first flight I could. I feared something was wrong and when I got to your apartment, you weren't answering. When I finally got in, I found you unresponsive on your couch."

I closed my eyes as I felt groggy and strange. "What happened to me?"

"You weren't completely healed. You developed a bleed in your brain. If I hadn't found you when I had, you could have died." He stroked my hair more as if the moment he stopped, I'd be gone. "I was just grateful that you survived."

Opening my eyes, I looked down. "Why do you care so much for me?" I looked away because I couldn't stand it if the truth was painful. He must still feel guilty over me for what happened in Egypt. "I free you from the guilt you feel over me."

He turned me to look at him. His eyes filed with emotion. "It isn't guilt that makes me care for you." He smiled at me, though it wasn't his carefree one that I had gotten used to. "I've never met anyone like you. A woman so curious about everything. You wish to learn yet haven't been able to. I want to help you and be your friend. Not because of guilt or pity, but because of your passion for life."

I started to feel sleepy again. "But no one wants me. Not even... my... parents..." My mind drifted away as my words turned into just a soft puff of air.

~*~*~

I stroked the white tiger who laid next to me so very content, though she's been restless throughout the day. "I miss him too." My eyes going to the pale blue moon. "He's been gone two full moons and here I lay pining for him."

"I wish never for you to pine for me."

A gasped rushed out as I shot up and looked over to the door. Horus stood there smiling. He was freshly bathed and oiled. "Forgive me for keeping you waiting a tad longer than you should have. I felt you deserved a clean warrior that came back to you."

I rose and went over to him. He smiled more but I pouted. "You wish not for me to have the honor to care for you?" His confidence faltered. I let my fingers trail over his bronzed skin walking away. "But if you wish other women to honor you, I understand."

He grabbed my hand as it and spun me back to him. His hands skimming down my back. "I just wish for you to not worry about such things." I yelped when he lifted me up into the air. "There is one thing no mortal woman in the world could do for me." He looked deep into my eyes laying me down upon my bed. "Love me completely."

~*~*~

I woke to the feeling of someone moving me. I found myself draped on a wheelchair. My body felt stronger, but I was still very weak. My eyes opened and focused to see that we were at the front entrance.

"How is our schedule? Will we be on time for our flight?" Siris lifted me up from the wheelchair and into a town car that had been waiting just outside of the front entrance.

My hand rose and touched his arm before he could pull it away from me. "Flight?"

Siris took my hand seeing I was awake now. "Yes. I can't in good conscious let you stay and let some dark fool kill you. You are in need of a long rest to fully recover."

My eyes started to droop. "But..."

I heard him chuckle as he sat on the seat next to me int he back of the town car. "No buts. Just rest more. I'm going to take care of you and see that you recover completely." I couldn't protest as I fell back to sleep leaning against his side.

~*~*~

My hands gripped the side of the pool. Horus moved my hips slowly so his member was fully and completely within me. It's full length known to me as I never want it any different way. I knew exactly where he was within me.

"I wish nothing more than to stay in your arms. To make you know how much I love you." Horus whispered into my ear as he slowly pulled out of me and then back over him. "I wish one day that we might have a child of our own. One as gloriously beautiful as you."

I smiled. "A child. You already thinking of a child?"

"I thought it the whole time I was gone." His lips graced my earlobe. "Please. Let's make a child. My goddess." To emphasis his desire, he did the one thing he knew causes me the most pleasure. The quick shift of his hips made me moan.

"Ahh... When is the next time you go back into battle?"

He hesitated for a heart beat before he sighed. "In three days time."

I slid away from him and he let me. "That wouldn't be enough time to even start the process to conceive a child."

He glided over to me and cupped my face with one of his hands. "I'm yours for as long as you need for the process. The pharaoh has given me the permission to do as I wish till midnight in three nights." Horus smiled. "He knows of my desire and wishes for me to know that kind of happiness."

I sighed softening. "You discussed this?"

Horus nodded. "Nights have been long and lonely. Men talk."

"As do women." I blushed. "Your mother has come to visit me several times."

He nodded. "I know." He smiled and kissed my blushing cheeks. "My father saw me." He kissed my lips. "I think they've been talking and plotting together."

I laughed. "Are they plotting for a grandchild?"

He laughed too. "I do believe that is what they have been doing."

~*~*~

My stomach grumbled loudly and I felt like I was going to be sick. I was nauseous and dizzy. My head felt funny. This was not a delightful state to come around in. All I wanted to do was be knocked back out.

My eyes drifted to the window. There were clouds outside. We were still in the air and I was in a private plane. Flying away from my tortured life. Away from everything I've known.

"Here." I looked over and found Siris holding a bowl of soup. He spooned some of it out of the bowl and offered it to me. "You've had very little to eat lately and were in the hospital for quite a long time."

Taking the spoonfuls he gave me, I looked at him. "How long?" All I remembered was waking a few times but nothing more than that.

He frowned as he offered me more soup. "A week."

I touched his arm looking at him. "You stayed with me for a whole week?"

He nodded. "Of course. You're my friend who needed someone by your side when you needed them the most."

I didn't say anything as he helped me eat the rest of the soup. I was just so hungry and weak. His eyes told me that he didn't like how silent I was at the moment. That he knew I mustn't have many friends that would do that. None actually. But I wasn't about to tell him that and get pity from him.

Two sets of bodies hopped onto my lap. I looked down and found my two cats looking up at me worried. "Sorry to worry you both." My hands weakly lifting up to pet each of them.

Siris tilted his head to the side. "You can tell how they're feeling?"

My shoulders lifted and fell. I knew I was a bit of a freak, but I have been this way my whole life. "They're my babies." My two cats started to rub all across my front.

"You know, out of all the ancient Egyptian gods, Bastet was the only one that could do that. Though cats were her forte, she could read anyone and any animal as if she felt it herself. One of many reasons she was so loved."

I frowned at him and he smiled at me. He tapped my nose. "Now just relax. I believe the Gods are still around us and looking out for us."

My eyes rose to Horus who was looking right at me looking a bit lost. I knew one God of old that was real. Could others be really out there? Was it that we just didn't see them?

I frowned. "I've been having these dreams all my life. Dreams of a man who was strong and yet gentle. A warrior. Only recently they have changed. He's the same, but now..." I looked at Siris. "The dream me calls him Horus."

Siris took my hand and turned it over seeing the tattoo. "It could be just the branding. The mind can make certain things up and let you imagine your most deepest fantasies be something you've been told. Twisting your reality." He placed his hand over my tattoo covering it from me.

I felt my heart constrict. My eyes went up to Horus, but he was gone. Having him gone left a bit of a hole. I didn't feel so comfortable or easy without him nearby. I felt unprotected.

Siris slipped his hand away and Horus came back. But Horus didn't look so hot. He slipped against the wall breathing heavily. He even looked shaken, but he still he gave me a smile. "I am fine." He breathed as he tried to regain himself.

All I want to do was rush over to him and hold him. His eyes locked onto mine and he smiled as he misted away. Then his hand was on mine and he sat next to me. I wanted to know where he went and what happened, but having him next to me was all I needed to reassure me he was alright.

"You should rest more. We still have some time before we land." Siris shifted and sat across from me. He laid down across the length of the two with his leg stretching out so his heels rested on the seat across the way.

I frowned. "You can't be comfortable like that."

He smiled glancing over. "I'm more than used to this." He adjusted slightly. "I fly so much for my profession." I watched as he yawned and then relaxed falling asleep right there.

"He speaks truly. Sleep. I have you." Horus pulled me down to lay my head on his lap. "Sleep." His voice whispered down to me. I obeyed as he lightly brushed the tattoo that was visible where my hand rested palm up in front of my face.

~*~*~

I looked down at my stomach, and touched it as a smile danced across my face. My heart overflowing with joy. So much was making my eternal existence perfect beyond imagining.

A child. A child of Horus'. Something we created together. Something that showed how much we love each other. How our love overflows into a living creation.

I looked down to all the cats lounging about. "Would you all think I could be a great mother?" All the cats smiled and meowed happily confirming they thought so.

My smile grew even more. "I hope so."

Chapter Five

My eyes went wide as I looked up to the ceiling of the grand foyer. A glittering chandelier sending light everywhere. Siris having to hold me up seeing his place then moment we got inside. The front had shocked me, but it didn't look so big from the outside. "You're letting me stay here?" That was all I could ask.

Siris laughed helping my shaking legs self farther into the... MANSION!!! "And you may always stay if you find you cannot bare to leave. I do have a fully ready studio apartment in a building all to itself. Grand kitchen, fully furnished. Though if you wanted, we could change anything out."

My hand gripped his jacket weakly as I started to feel dizzy again. "You might want to stop. Didn't the doctor say something about shock not being good for me?"

He lifted me up into his arms as I continued to struggle. "Forgive me. I got carried away with my daydreaming out loud." He smiled at me with a bit of concern laced in his features. "Too much?"

"Just a little bit." I told him as he set me down on a couch in what looked to me like a family room off the kitchen where there were two ladies fixing something. He placed me so I was half laying down, half sitting up with my shoulder blades resting against pillows of the armrest.

He chuckled with a smile as one of the ladies came over with two plates. She set down the plates on the coffee table before vanishing into the kitchen again. Siris lifted up my legs and sat down draping my legs over his lap. He leaned over and grabbed the plates handing me one as he got comfortable.

"I'll give you a tour after we eat." He smiled at me before taking a bite of the Philly steak that he had on his plate.

I smiled too as I bit into mine. It was like I had growing up. When I could have afforded it that is. I remember the man who owned the sub shop down the road from the house. He was nice and always gave me a discount. Not to mention the free bag of chips. There were even times he let me helped out when he was slammed with customers. Those were the days I got my meals free for my hard work as I was technically underage working there.

I popped a potato chip into my mouth as I looked at Siris. "Do you have these whenever you come back home?"

He laughed around his bite. He shrugged swallowing his latest bite. "Some times I just need something so..."

"Deliciously unhealthy?"

He smiled. "Exactly. Jilliann makes the best cheese steaks."

"The young master is always so sweet." The elder of the two ladies from the kitchen came into the room. She looked to be about in her fifties. Her hair was white with a dark reddish spot from her temples.

Siris frowned. "You know how I hate being called master." He smiled guiltily at me. "Been called it all my life." He shook his head. "Most of my wealth comes from my father."

"And he's been asking us forever to just call him Siris, but his father had always told us not to." She smiled at him tapping his foot lightly. "Old habits are hard to kill even when the heir becomes the successor. Good to have you back."

He smiled. "Good to be back." He turned to me. "And to have my friend's health back up."

I pouted and Jilliann smiled. "I'm glad our young master has found someone to treat right." My face went scarlet thinking she was saying that Siris was interested in me like that.

Siris groaned letting his head fall back against the back of the couch. "Jilliann! She's not that kind of friend. She's a sister type of friend."

Jilliann frowned as she looked at me. "But she's so pretty and how you bolted out to the airport after you talked with her on the phone that I just thought..."

Siris shook his head. "True she is beautiful, but I feel no romantic feelings to her." He smiled at me. "Sorry Bea. You're just not my type."

There was a smile on my face as held up my hands. "As with me. Not wanting to jump you in the slightest."

I saw Horus out of the corner of my eye relax. He was worried for some reason that I might find Siris...desirable. A God worrying over me. This was such a new feeling. Two guys caring for me and looking out for me.

Horus, though no one saw him, stayed off to the side when there were others around me. He only did that after I told him it was very distracting if he touched me and no one else could see him doing it. How can you explain something like that to anyone? You just can't without looking insane.

My hand came up and covered the yawn that forced it's way out. Siris tugged my legs so I found myself laying down. "Sleep Bea. You need more rest. I'll have my doctor come check you out when you wake. Take a nice nap." He tossed the throw that was on the back of the couch over me.

I drifted to sleep as I felt fingers grace my cheek lightly. "He's right. You had a long flight and the past week has been hard on you." Horus' voice whispered into my ear as he touch my cheek more.

~~~

"Must you?" My eyes looking weary at the man before me.

The slightly older gentleman looked up at me and grinned tightly holding the needle in his gloved hands. "Afraid so dear. Mr. Denton has instructed me to take very good care of you. Knowing everything about you can help with many things." He smiled at me. "I can even tell Jilliann any dietary requirements you may need."

I pouted as he slid the needle into my arm. Horus was in the corner glaring at the poor doctor. It was only because I told him no when he wanted to hurt the poor man that the good doctor was even still alive. "It's not right that they draw your blood. They're taking a part of you."

The doctor took the needle out and pulled the vile off placing a cap on it. He then labeled it and placed it in a plastic bag. "I will have the results back by tomorrow afternoon and I'll know if everything is alright then." He smiled at me. "But don't worry, I think you're just fine after a bit more resting and relaxing."
~~~

He stood. "As the doctors at the hospital said, take it easy and just relax." His assistant placed a bandaid on my arm where the good doctor had taken my blood. "You'll hear from me tomorrow, or should I say Master Denton will hear from me and relay anything I find out."

I thanked him and his assistant for coming to see me. Siris would have been here with me if he hadn't gotten an urgent call from the university about a display of the Bubastis excavation that they are preparing for once things get approved through their channels. He told me that he told everyone to treat me like his sister and if anyone upset me, he'd know and deal with it with a vengeance. I had pouted at him which made him laugh just before he walked out the front door.

The doctor left and Jilliann came in with some clothes in her hands. "Did it go well?"

I smiled and nodded. "Very well. I never liked doctors but I like him. He has a wonderful bedside manner." And made me feel very comfortable to let him do what he needed to. I wasn't even as upset when he drew my blood as I normally was.

Jilliann smiled back at me placing the clothes in my lap. "That's very good to hear. Now..." She put her hands on her hips. "The young master has made me promise that you had to relax. My first thought was for you to enjoy the hot tub."

She walked to the door. "I'll be back in a little after you change into your outfit." She smiled as she paused at the door. "I hope you don't mind that I asked my daughter to offer you a swimsuit. The master said you didn't have an outfit and you're about her size."

I looked down at the clothes when she closed the door. There wasn't just a swimsuit. But a wrap dress too. They were both her daughter's no doubt. It felt strange having people being so nice to help me out like they were all doing.

Looking around, I found Horus laying on the bed looking a bit bored now that the doctor was gone and he didn't have anything to occupy him. "Are you going to join me?"

He looked over at me and shrugged. "As I can't seem to find any of the other Gods, that would be nice."

I frowned at him. "You've been looking?"

He looked back up to the ceiling. "Yes. When I leave your side, I'm searching for them. Even if they can't see me, I still want to know they're alive after all this time."

I went over to him and sat next to him. "They can't see you?"

He shook his head. "You are the only one in all the world." His eyes came to me. "You're the only one who can see me, hear me, and feel me. I've been cursed by Ra to this fate." He rose and cupped my cheek in his hand. "When you fell, I felt that you were a sign that I'm being given the opportunity to prove I was imprisoned unjustly. That I was framed for the crime I was punished for."

I tilted my head more into his hand. "Please tell me what happened."

He sighed heavily as he rose. I followed him as he looked out the window. "I was returning from war beside the Pharaoh. I rode hard and fast to my beloved. Every ounce of my being more than needing her touch and love."

He closed his eyes. "My beloved was the Goddess Bastet. We were tied together for six of your years. She was and still is the love of my immortal soul."

He turned to me glaring. "And she was murdered." Storming over to me, he gripped my upper arms. Anger and rage in his eyes. "I was blamed for her death and sentenced to endless loneliness in the pure darkness below the ruins of her destroyed temple where she died."

His anger vanished and his legs gave out leaving him on his knees before me. He rested his forehead on my sternum. "I felt her death. The moment her body turned to ash in the flames..."

I pushed him away and stared at him in shock. My own legs gave out and I fell to the floor looking at him. The images of the one nightmare I'm had coming back to me over and over. "The only way for a God to die is for them not to have a physical body."

He tilted his head to the side crawling over to me. "How do you know that?" There was an underlining threat in his voice.

"Horus!" I froze as Horus shot his head to someone behind me. The voice was deep and dark, but there was a kindness to it too. "You are frightening her, son."

Horus rose up off me and I felt someone pulled me gently off the floor. "Father." Horus whispered staring at the person next to me.

I looked and came face to face with the man from my nightmare. No, the God from my nightmare and who tried to sooth me. "Osiris." Tears sprang to my eyes and I crumpled into him sobbing.

"Shh child, I know. I've missed you too. Forgive me for taking so long to find you in this life." Osiris cooed into my ear trying to sooth me.

I looked at him and he looked down at me with those red eyes that didn't frighten me. They were soothing and eased my soul. "You've been searching for me?"

He smiled as he nodded. "Of course. Ever since I set you free to be reborn, I've been looking for you with all my heart."

"Ask him..."

"Why?" I asked even with Horus telling me to from behind me. I really wasn't paying that much attention to him at the moment. Not with another God right here in front of me from my dreams.

Osiris took me over to the bed which was to be mine while I was here. "You are very important to me." He took my hands in his as he looked down to them. "I know my son was framed. That Ra, in his state of pure grief and rage, punished him without knowing all of what happened."

"But I'm no one." Horus sat down behind me and pressed his back against mine as I said that. His presence alone telling me I was someone now. That somehow Fate decided I was someone so very special.

Osiris cupped my cheek. His dark robes shifted around him and moving away from his pure white arm. "But you are someone. Someone so special as to be able to help my son gain his honor again." I lowered my head, but he brought it back up. "You're the only one who can. You have the memories to help him." Horus shifted to look at his father, but Osiris couldn't see him. "He needs you more than even he can understand at the moment."

Horus shifted again and I saw him try to touch his father, but his hand passed right through his father's white skin. Horus turned his back on us and walked a little away after rising from behind me. "What does it matter anyways? Bastet is gone."

I frowned at Horus. "Would you not want to know the true person or God that killed her to pay?" All I wanted in that moment was the vengeful God Horus had been earlier.

He turned his head to the side but didn't look at me. "She was my world, my sun. Without her, I'm always in darkness."

I rose, but Osiris held me back. "You cannot change his mind when he thinks a certain way. Best to let him be for the time."

"You heard him?"

Osiris shook his head. "No, just your expression and the pain his words caused."

Horus looked over to me with unreadable eyes. Then he turned away and misted somewhere else as he did from time to time. It hurt to see him so upset. He was so caring that he doesn't deserve the pain thrusted at him. A pain that someone else caused maliciously. A pain I never want to see him in, but didn't know how to stop.

I sat down heavily looking at my hands. "He doesn't deserve so much pain."

Osiris pulled me to him and stroked my hair. "Nor have you." He sighed. "The moment you stepped in Bubastis, I saw you. Then I found out what your life has been like." He kissed the top of my head. "The fates have been too cruel with you."

I looked up at him. The God that I've known through my dreams and who was like my father to me even if this was the first time I got to meet him fully. "What did I do in my previous life that was so bad?"

His eyes turned down. "Nothing dear child. All who go through the waters of rebirth are cleansed of their previous life." He hugged me a little more. "The pain life brings is done by another." He moved a strand of hair that fell in front of my eye. "But now you don't have to fear anything. I'll be looking out for you and see that you know very little pain."

I tilted my head to the side. "But you must have very important responsibilities." Much more important than looking out for one lone mortal like me.

He smiled tapping my nose playfully. "You are my delightful responsibility at the moment."

Looking down at my outfit, he smiled with a mischievous look. He lifted his robe and covered me to my neck. His robe feeling indescribably soft and silky like nothing else I've felt before. So eerily soothing and comfortable. When his robe fell away, I was wearing the bikini and wrap dress. "I cannot slow time for much longer and have kept you from changing."

My heart sank a bit thinking of Horus and how he said he was going to join me in the hot tub. But he was gone and I don't think he'd be joining me in the hot tub now. "I don't think I'm in the mood for that now."

Osiris smiled a little, though strained slightly as it was. "I have a feeling, she won't let you." He misted away leaving me alone in my room puzzling over his words.

I jumped a little when there was a knock on the door before it opened. Jilliann came in and smiled till she saw the look on my face. "Are you feeling alright dear?"

I looked out the window. "I don't feel like going now."

She marched over to me and pulled me up from the edge of my bed delicately for my injured state. "Nonsense. You need to relax. Just looked at you. Tight as a harp's string." Her hand squeezed my shoulder letting me feel just how tight my shoulders really were. A small bit of pain came with her squeezing showing me how deep my muscles had tightened.

I had no choice but to let her drag me to a giant room that had an Olympic style swimming pool and a floor to ceiling wall of windows. Jilliann pulled me over to a twelve person hot tub already bubbling away. It was in the center of the back wall raised up a bit from the surface of the pool.

At the hot tub, in a flash Jilliann had the wrapped dress I was wearing off and draped over a lounge chair nearby. She even pushed me up the stairs gently and nudged me into the hot tub. I was hit with a soothing scent of sage that had me inhaling deeply. It was already unwinding me.

"I'll be right back with some snacks and a cocktail for you." She hurried as she left. Somehow she must have known that I was about to refuse the cocktail.

I sighed as I sat back and let the bubbles dance around me. My body feeling greedy as it wanted to stay right here forever. Closing my eyes, I let the heat seep into me. I needed this more than I thought I would have.

A gasp slipped out as a hand lifted up my foot. Horus was in the hot tub with me. His hands working the tight muscles of my foot and calf. He frowned. "Do you know no days of rest?"

I looked out the window at the setting sun and shrugged. "I had no time to rest or could afford such a luxury."

"Now you can."

I looked back over to him and his eyes were only on my leg as he draped it across his lap and worked higher. "Are you alright?"

He shook his head. "Forgive me for tying you to me without permission."

I started to move to him, but Jilliann choose that moment to come back. "Here we go dear. A pitcher of my refreshing adult pink lemonade and my favorite tiny fruit tarts. They're small enough that each are just one bite."

"You didn't have to make so many for me."

"Not just you." I smiled as Siris came jogging in with his trunks on.

"Did everything go alright?"

He rolled his eyes as he hopped into the tub and sank down. "Sometimes I wonder about my students and their commonsense level." I pouted and he laughed. "See why I wish you were my student. You aren't an idiot like they are. Their emergency was that they thought one piece went one place and another went somewhere else. I left written instructions that were more than clear."

"Here you go young master." Jilliann handed Siris a glass of her alcoholic pink lemonade. "Now I expect you to be a gentleman and not drink the whole pitcher. Lady Bea deserves at least half of it."

"Am I even allowed that much with my head injury and all?"

Jilliann frown. "Alright a quarter. I'll see you both in the morning. Midnight snack is in the oven if you need it."

"Thank you Jilliann." Siris shouted after her as she left. He was smiling brightly. "She's been like a mother to me."

I raised an eyebrow at Siris as Horus seemed to be thinking while he continued to work my legs under the water where Siris couldn't see. Odd to feel comfortable like this. "Midnight snack?"

He chuckled drinking his pink lemonade smiling. "A growing boy needed food at any moment." He stretched over to the tray of tarts. "I was no exception to the rule." He grinned popping one into his mouth.

I giggled at both Siris and Horus. Horus had tickled my foot and he knew it. He was grinning a bit. A mischievous grin that was much better than his serious face.

Shaking my head at both of them, I took a tart too. It was so good. Apple and rhubarb tart. It was sweet and tart at the same time. The sweetness was more natural than added sugar. It was just so perfect when paired with this pink lemonade.

We soaked in the hot tube sipping on our drinks and talking. He told stories of different digs he's done or been apart of throughout his career. I listened to everything feeling happy to know him now. He told great stories. I bet he was an amazing professor.

"Come on you. I think the alcohol has made you sleepy." Siris put his hands under me and lifted me up. He set me down on a lounge chair before grabbing a towel. "Or maybe it was my stories."

I shook my head groggily as he dried me off slightly before wrapping the towel around me. "I want to hear more stories." I sighed. "I love those stories." More than loved because they made me feel like I was there with him.

He smiled drying himself off with his own towel. "Then tomorrow you shall hear more. I'm afraid it will be later in the day like today, but not nearly as late. I have to go back in for the morning classes and teach. The life of a tenured professor at a respectable university."

"Umm... I want to go with." I smiled sleepily.

He laughed. "Okay Miss very tipsy. If you're alright in the morning, you can come with me. The second you get bored, my driver can bring you back."

I smiled letting my head hang back. "College!"

"Wow. That stuff really got you good. And only three glasses." He chuckled.

"You drank the rest. Why aren't you gone?"

"That's because I've built up a tolerance for alcohol."

He laid me down on my bed and slid me under the covers as if he'd done it for years. "You know this will be the third time I've gone to sleep today." I yawned as I shifted to my side cuddling one of the pillows.

"Yes and you've needed all of them. Now sleep and I'll see you in the morning." I felt my cats pounce onto the bed and laid down with me. They have been exploring the whole mansion since the moment we got here. I bet they found several great spots to lay down in for the daylight hours.

Siris leaned down and kissed my forehead. "Good night my kitty cat." He whispered to me just before I was gone from the world. His little pet name following me into my dreams.

Chapter Six

I smiled as I spun around in Siris' desk chair behind his solid oak professor's desk. He laughed as he looked through his mail. "You look like a little kid in daddy's chair in his study."

A giggle came out as I stopped the chair using the edge of his beautiful desk. "I always wanted to do that with one of these chairs for forever. One not in a store." I sat straight up and folded my hands together. "So, when's class starting?"

He smiled opening one of his large envelops. "In two hours. First I need to grade a few tests they took on friday." His eyes looking through the papers that were in a large envelop.

"Anything I can help with?" I hated not being of any use and not busy. Not after all the years I spent working for Seth Dath.

Siris smiled leaning over the desk and turned on his computer. "Can you check my e-mail for me and see if any of my students sent me anything important? You can tell what is from a student as there will be a yellow flag next to their name. The red flags are for my bosses and the blue from co-workers. Any from the archeologist community will have purple flags." He smiled. "Just look for the yellow flags for now."

I smiled back so very happy to be doing anything to help him out for allowing me to come with him. "I can do that."

He chuckled taking a seat on one of the leather guest seats as he opened a huge folder that was on top of a stack of folders. He started going through page by page shaking his head. I smiled as I looked at a few e-mails that came in with yellow flags. Nothing really of note as two were just students wanting to know their test scores.

By the time he was a quarter of the way through the slack in front of him, he was getting up. "Time to get over to the other building where the class is. I'll need to set up for today's discussion."

I hopped up from his chair. "What can I carry?"

Shaking his head, he handed me his leather bag he carries with him everywhere. "You take care of my laptop while I'll get the box." He bent down and picked up a heavy looking box.

We walked over to the elevator and I pushed the button for the ground level. Every few seconds someone was walking by and saying hello to Siris as we waited. He nodded his head and returned their greetings. A few would stop and chat for him for a second before rushing off to their own tasks they were doing. Everyone seemed to love Siris or were just so nice.

He raised an eyebrow at me in the elevator. "Why did you hide behind me when someone said hi?"

I blushed looking down shrugging. "I was nervous."

He chuckled as the door opened and we started out of the building. "Than I was glad to have been your shield. I hope in time you will become comfortable here enough that you'd say hello back to people."

"I think I just need a little time to adjust." I opened the door to the building he directed us to and he smiled walking in as I trailed behind him.

Earlier when I was getting ready to leave, Horus had told me he was going to try and find his father. He had been excited knowing he was still alive. Even if he couldn't touch or speak to him, to know where to find his father was all Horus had wanted. And I had encouraged him seeing some life back into that very unearthly handsome face of his.

When we entered the classroom, I was in awe. The classroom was really a small amphitheater. There were stadium seating with built-in desks. A large screen with a projector behind a stage where Siris was walking to. Off to the side of the stage was a desk with all sorts of things waiting to be used along with several buttons to be pushed.

Siris looked up at me with a smirk. "You can sit at the desk and pull my laptop out. After I set up everything, I'll show you what I'd like for you to do during the lesson." I snapped out of my gawking as I skipped down the steps to the desk.

As his laptop booted up, I watched as he set up several tables draping a cloth over them from the box. Next he opened several boxes placing the tops on the tables and what was in those boxes on top of the lids. In front of each object, he placed something small that liked like a wireless camera. He was very wealthy so I wasn't ruling anything out.

I sat back when he came over. We laughed when he playfully tried to sit on my lap. Swiping at his rear, he shook his head while he did somethings on his laptop. All I could do was laugh. "And why don't you have a girlfriend?"

He shrugged. "I've had a good amount over the years, but none of them liked that I love my job more and how often I'm away. They tend to break up with me before I head out for a new dig site." He looked over his shoulder at me. "Why? You offering?" He wiggled his eyebrows at me suggestively.

I shrugged. "I thought I was the sister type to you. Not the type you find attractive in that way."

He shrugged too. "That's what I told Jilliann." I could tell he wasn't being truthful about his feelings toward me. He finished and turned around leaning against the desk so his butt was up against the desk. "I will admit that I care deeply for you. But as for romantic feelings, those may come later after we figure everything out. The way we became friends was so sudden and intense that neither of us know what we are feeling. Just relax and know that if I really start feeling that way, I'll tell you. I'll be up front about everything."

Looking down, I nodded. He lifted my chin. "You okay?" Worry in his eyes as they searched mine.

Taking a deep breathe, I nodded again. "Yeah. I think I was worried for a bit."

He sighed. "I'm sorry I worried you for a second. That wasn't my intention." Then he smirked and wiggled his eyebrows at me again. "I guess I need to see about getting you laid to loosen you up."

I gasped in mock horror and swatted him away. "You will do no such thing! I don't need to get laid. Now go get ready for class. I got this now thank you very much." He laughed full heartedly as he went back over to the stage just as a bell rang and students started coming in. Each with books in their arms and discussing something among themselves.

Most of the girls made me roll my eyes internally. Their tops were lower than they should be showing off their chests to Siris. They were also sitting up front so he would see them. Of course they would want him. He was still young and very successful, not to mention good looking.

I made a paper ball and threw it at him. Siris laughed as he tossed it back before he came over. “Yes my assistant?” He folded his hand over the edge of the desk and leaned his chin on them. The desk top was shoulder height to someone on the stage.

Leaning over, I smirked giving him a kiss on the cheek. “Just had to see what all the wanting girls would do if I kissed your cheek.”

He stepped back, tilted his head to the side, and raised his eyebrow at me. “You trying to make my students jealous of you?”

I stuck my tongue out at him and he laughed just as the final bell rang. He turned back to his students. “Hello everyone. Last week was interesting and I wish to apologize to you all.” He turned to me. “As you all most likely noticed that I have a friend with me today. She’ll be helping me keep myself straight for you all as my assistant.”

Suppressing a giggle at all the relieved sighs from all the girls was quite funny. Siris just smiled and winked at a few girls. “Have no fear. Now that I’ve stolen her away from her awful boss, she’ll help keep me organized and better prepared to make each of my classes even better. Now...”

He turned to the table and lifted a remote pressing a button. The room dimmed except the tables and the projector turned on. On the laptop there were individual pictures of the objects. I adjusted the images so when Siris clicked to them, they were ready as he asked me to do for him.

For the whole class, he even had me spellbound about the subject of the pharaoh's lives and each of their families. Before the hour and a half was over, he had spoke about all the families. He just had a way with bringing the past to life. It also didn’t hurt that I had flashes of those actual pharaohs he spoke about.

“Are you thinking about me?” I jumped slightly as Horus’ whispered into my ear. Looking down at my wrist, I was outlining my tattoo. That’s why he was here. He thought I had called him.

Pulling out my cell, I pretended like I got a call. "Only a little." I whispered to him. He smiled as he sat on the desk allowing me to look up at him without people thinking I'm crazy.

He raised an eyebrow. "What made you think of me?"

I blushed and smiled. "Just listening to Siris' lecture on Pharaohs."

"And naturally you thought of me knowing I had once protected them." He looked over to the relics Siris had on display. "Will you find out for me when the last pharaoh ruled? I've come to know that they no longer rule over the Nile."

I smiled sweetly. "Of course. How was your search for your dad?"

He sighed laying down nearly across the whole desk. "I had thought he'd be back down below in the great hall of souls, but he wasn't. There was another down there directing souls. Guiding them into the pools to be cleansed and reborn into another life, or into paradise."

I frowned. "Maybe in time he'll show back up. I know that your father loves you and is trying to help clear you."

He nodded as he shifted on the desk and looked at the screen of Siris' laptop. "Is this what he has you doing at the moment?"

The house lights came up and I looked over at Siris as he told his students what to read for the next class as there was going to be a quiz. As the girls seemed to drool as he turned his backside toward them and started packing up all his artifacts. They all were shamelessly staring right at his rear.

"I should get back and close the laptop. Will I talk with you later?"

Horus looked at me and smiled. Shifting so he was on his side. "Are you acting like I'm on the other side of that device?" I rolled my eyes and pulled my phone away and put it in my pocket. Horus frowned. "Does that mean you can't talk to me now?"

Siris came over with the box of stuff and set it down right through Horus' crotch. I smiled trying not to laugh as Horus moved and the box was still between his legs where he sat on the desk.

"So how did you like the class?"

"I liked it very much. I wish I was in your class so I could ogle you with them hearing about the past as you weave the past for us on that silver tongue of yours."

Siris laughed as he closed his laptop and put it in his bag. "I like that. 'Silver tongue of mine.' I'll have to remember you like to listen to me talking." He smiled down at me looking very amused by my choice of words. "Would you like me to be your personal tutor?"

I frowned. "No you won't be *professor*."

Shaking his head, he lifted the box up and then draped his bag over my shoulder. He moved the box under one arm and laid the other over my shoulders. "Come on assistant, let's get back to my office before the line gets too longer of students that need to talk to me."

I blushed when Horus walked beside me and was glaring at the arm around my shoulders. He didn't look too happy that Siris was even touching me. "Does he have to touch you this way?"

In the building Siris had his office in, I excused myself to the bathroom. I gave Horus a look before I pulled out my phone again. A big smile lit my face. "Did someone get jealous?"

He growled. "A God doesn't become jealous of a mortal."

Taking a seat on the couch, I raised an eyebrow. "Are you sure about that? You had glared at just an arm. He was just being my friend. No reason to be jealous."

Horus growled as he towered over me. I just casually leaned back and looked up at him smiling at him. "There is no reason for me to be jealous of a mortal. He could never touch you like I can."

My eyes closed as I bit my lip. His hand caressed my face, down my neck, over my chest, and wrapped around my waist. In the wake of his touch, my skin tingled and those tingles slipped deeper into my body.

I felt Horus lean down as his breathe was next to my ear. "No mortal could touch you like this as only a God tied to you can make you feel this way. Only I can slip beneath your skin."

Clearing my throat, I took a deep breathe. "I should get back to Siris' office before he starts worrying that something happened to me." I moved out from under him as I put my phone away again leaving the restroom.

Back in the office, Siris raised an eyebrow as he sat in his chair talking with one of his students, a female student. I just blushed as my skin still tingled and went over to the chair in front of the window. He just shook his head as he went back helping his student with apparently had a paper that was going to be his advanced studies final.

Once in a while, Siris asked for my help with the students for the next two hours. Him perpetuating the impression that I was his assistant. When he walked out his twelfth student, he turned a small sign around with a big sigh of relief. "That's it for the office hours being open for students." He turned to me with a huge smile. "Shall we go get lunch now?"

I giggled as I set down the pile of papers on the smaller glass 'student' desk that was in here in front of a window. I've kind of claimed it as my desk as his assistant. I was at the moment trying to organize all his paperwork that was just piled up behind his desk on the bookshelves. He was in serious need of an assistant more than I thought.

"How did you function with all these papers jumbled together?"

He laughed as he opened the door for me. "I told you I needed someone to help me. Now you see why." He pinched my cheek. "And it is so very cute of you for already jumping in and getting your feet wet."

Smacking his hand away, I laughed. "I was taking pity on you, you helpless oaf!"

He gasped just before I found myself tossed over his shoulder. "And just for that, I'll have to punish you." The next thing I knew was that Siris was asking any male students that he came across to smack my rear. I yelped with each smack as some were a bit too hard for it to be fun.

After about the tenth smack, he called off the guys and set me down on my feet. I pouted crossing my arms at him. I wasn't about to let him know my butt hurt and was most likely bright red. When a hand slipped over the sore orbs and the skin started tingling, I didn't waver knowing it was Horus healing it by his touch.

"That wasn't nice."

Siris smiled faking innocence. "How about I make it up to you?" He took my hand and started out of the building to his very expensive sports car. Of course my jaw had dropped this morning when he showed me his garage and the twenty, yes twenty, cars. All the cars were high-end ones at that with a few pristine vintage cars mixed in.

"Where are we going?" I wasn't about to waver slipping into his sleek and beautiful car.

Siris smirked. "You'll see."

Chapter Seven

Siris had his phone out and talking to someone on the other end as he drove. I didn't care as I leaned against the seat in his car. Too tired from the delicious five course lunch he treated me to at a very expensive restaurant. Of course after such a posh lunch, I was tired and sleepy. Hence Siris on his phone calling for his on-the-call driver to come pick me up and take me back to his place.

"You shouldn't have made me eat so much." I moaned out groggily.

He laughed closing his phone. "But you enjoyed yourself, didn't you?" His mouth curling into a grin that reminded me of the cheshire cat, so sneaky and conning.

A yawn slipped out and I covered my mouth with my hand. No need to forgo manners even when I was so tired. "Yes, but now I'm so sleepy." Okay, that may not have been so lady-like to whine like that.

"And that's exactly why I have my driver coming to pick you up when we pull into my parking spot. He'll take you to the house and even carry you up to your bed if you're completely out of it." Which I don't doubt I will be because of the lunch he made me have. Well, not *made* me have.

I pouted. "I don't have to go back. You have a leather couch in your office that looked very cozy. I could always take a nap there." This couldn't be the end of my first ever time at a college. A real life university. It was too soon.

He shook his head. "Sorry, Bea. The university won't allow me to leave you sleeping in my office nor would I when I'm not there. The phone rings all the time as I've found out once trying to nap. It'd be best if you rested back at the house." His hand went into mine and gave me a squeeze. "You also need to relax a little more. You've aided me enough for one day."

Another yawn. “But there’s still so much that I need to do.” Some many papers still spread out across that little glass desk that need to be sorted and filed properly.

Lifting up my hand, he kissed it softly across my knuckles. “You will have the chance to finish later. There’s no time limit for you to get everything done today. You didn’t have to do what you’ve done already.”

“But it’s to help you.” Sleep was really tugging at me and I knew he could hear it in my voice. My eyes wouldn't even open now to look at him.

He chuckled kissing my hand again. “And you’ll get back to it tomorrow. I can’t let you over do anything as I’ve been charged with looking out for you, and making you relax is part of that.”

“Big meanie.” I grumbled and Siris chuckled deeply while I drifted to sleep right there in his passenger seat.

~~~

What woke me wasn’t being lifted from either two cars or being taken to bed. What really woke me up was someone softly tracing the features of my face. The feel of a very masculine body draped beside me with him on his side. His whole body making sure he wouldn’t disturb my sleep.

I felt him lean down as his breathe fanned out across my ear and neck. The warmth heating my skin and a soft shiver went down my spine to my toes. “I know you’re waking my beautiful mortal.”

A smile lifted at the corners of my mouth before he laughed out loud with my swift movement. I had rolled over him and now I was draped over Horus’ front. Wiggling a little till I was comfortable. If he was going to call me mortal, I was going to use him as a body pillow just to get back at him. He maybe a God, but he tied himself to me.

“Why am I being used in this way?” He laughed. “I’m a God and should not be taking this from you. Though you are my mortal.”

I moved again to stretch out over him smiling. “It was your own fault for waking me.” And it was. It was his body against mine that lured me back to reality.
~~~

His chest vibrated and I bounced a little with his laugh. “So that is why you have caged me under you?”

“Yes.” I giggled as he shifted a little to get comfortable.

His arms wrapped around my waist and held me to him. “Then I will hold you captive in return.” A gasped as he twisted us around so swiftly that I barely felt a thing. “And now you are full captured.”

I opened my eyes and looked up at him. “You’re being very playful.” I smiled. “I actually like it when you are.”

He pouted. “But this and earlier are the only times I’ve been *this* way with you.”

I returned his pout. “Don’t you remember what your dad said when he was here?”

Horus’ eyes darkened. “How had I forgotten for a moment that you have memories that will help me? But what memories you could have that would help me?”

I looked away from his face. “I have her memories.”

Horus moved my head back till he was looking into my eyes again. His jaw clenching. “Whose memories?” His voice dripping with a threat of pain if I evaded. Trembling under him, he seemed to cool a fraction. He released my face as he softened his eyes. “Forgive me, I meant no harm to you.”

I took a deep shaking breathe. “I’ve had them all my life. They’ve given me comfort from the pain I experienced.” Horus’ whole body relaxed from its previously tense self to now trying to comfort me. “I never thought they were real memories, just dreams to help me. Dreams of someone to love me or who I was in them.” Tears slipped down my face. “I had always wished I was her for real.”

“Who?” He asked softly.

“Bastet.” I whispered as all my emotions poured out of me.

He took my wrist the tattoo was on and kissed the tattoo. My emotions leveled off as I felt his own slip into me from my wrist. A feeling of being protected and cherished just like in my dreams. “Shh, sweet mortal. I’m here now. Tell me these memories.” He smiled when he looked at me. “I wish to know what you know.”

A soft blush creeped up my cheek. “I know you two were tied to each other.” I looked down. “That you would be with her still had she not died.” That part might have hurt the worst. That I wouldn't know him or be tied to him like we were if she lived.

He lifted my chin. “We cannot change that and I have you now.”

I nodded. “I also know that you had tried for a child with her for three whole days for that was all you had been given by the Pharaoh at the time.”

He smiled sadly. “I never got to know if we succeeded.”

Slipping out from under him, I went to the window. Taking a deep breathe, I turned back to Horus. “I don’t know if I should tell you then.”

He looked at me as if he saw why. He looked gutted completely. “She was with child, our child, wasn’t she?” I nodded. He cupped his face as his pain doubled. “And she thought I had sent someone to kill her.”

I went over to him and wrapped him in my arms. “She never really believed it even as Osiris led her into the pool of souls. Her heart wouldn’t let her.”

He looked at me and I think this was the first time he had tears falling down his face in front of someone else. “You saw her death?”

I nodded. “It was so painful as I felt every bit of it like I was reliving it with her.” Lifting my arm to him as the skin started turning red as the memory took partial hold for a moment.

He gripped my arm and looked at it then at me as his eyes roamed over my face. Everything went hazy as he draped me over his arm. His hand cupping my cheek. “How had I not seen before?”

“I feel dizzy.” My arms felt like dead weights falling to the ground. I couldn’t even feel my legs.

“Sorry. That’s a bit of a side affect to peering into a mortal’s soul though yours seems different than many other’s I have seen.” He moved my hair out of my face. “But I have been out of the mortal world for a very long time. A mortal’s body could have changed drastically over that time.”

I frowned at him. “What are you talking about?”

He raised an eyebrow. “If I could, I would see into the soul of another to see if every mortal’s physical makeup was closer to that of a

God such as myself. It could be that your race is about to make a leap to the celestial like my kind had."

My frown deepened. "Is that possible?" Every part of my body starting to come back to me.

He shrugged. "Given enough time and for a race to change, anything is possible. Even spontaneous immortality from one generation to the next."

My head tilted to the side. "Is that how the Gods came into being? They spontaneously became immortal from their parents?"

He laughed. "I, no. My father and mother, yes."

I blushed. "Oh right, Osiris and Isis."

My blush went down to my toes. "What is the deal with my stomach always growling now?" I pointed my finger at Horus. "Before I meet you and you tied me to you, I never had my stomach growl so loudly before."

"Dun-tah-dah! I bring forth dinner for you milady!" My door flung open to reveal Siris there with a tray.

I humphed as I landed on the floor. Siris had startled me and I fell off of Horus' lap much to Horus' amusement. Siris set down the tray and came over to me. "You alright?"

Nodding, I yawned. "Sorry. I just woke up and then you came in. Guess I hadn't gotten my bearings yet."

He smiled. "Glad to see I was right in having my driver bring you home. You've slept for a good four hours."

Standing up, I stretched. "I blame that restaurant you took me to for lunch."

Siris laughed. "Than I'm so happy to had taken you."

I raised an eyebrow and pointed a finger at him. "I'm getting a terribly bad feeling that you're thinking about taking me to that restaurant again." I folded my hands across my chest and cocked my head with a slight tilt. I ignored Horus' shocked intake of air. "I forbid you to take me to that place again for lunch." I held a finger up when Siris smiled and opened his mouth. "And no other overly lavish restaurant for that matter. I will not have you make me that sleepy again."

Siris pouted and looked like a teenager that I knew he hadn't been for a long time. "Please. There are so many other restaurants that I can take you to. So many others that you've never tried before." He got down on his knees with his clasped hands raised to me making him look younger than a teenager begging and pleading to not have his toys taken away from him. "Pretty please my beautiful Bea."

I felt myself softening as my arms fell to my side. "But I just said no." My voice had lost all its authority and became so small in that one moment.

Siris slowly rose cupping my cheek so now he looked down on me. "Please. Let me shower you with all that has been denied such a woman with the most amazing soul I've ever seen. The soul of a Goddess."

I blinked and took a step. His eyes seemed to change or flash to another color that I couldn't put my finger on. "What did you just say?"

He frowned and his brows knitted together. "That you're perfect and should be treated like a Goddess. What's wrong?"

"You had said I had a soul of a Goddess." My words hung in the air.

He smiled stepping forward to cup my cheek again with his hand. His other going to my waist to prevent me to move away from him again. "Because you're so wonderful that if anyone was a Goddess you would be."

I felt myself sigh as he slid his other hand farther around my waist and he pulled me closer to him. My eye lids became heavier and my thoughts hazy as new emotions started to com to the surface. I didn't know what was happening in that moment. Even with him slowly leaning down.

A growl behind me made me jump. I jumped right out of Siris' arms and he seemed to blink out of his haze just as I was. He rubbed his face a few times trying to clear the thoughts that were in his mind away. "Sorry. I don't know what came over me for the moment."

I felt the blush heating over my cheeks from embarrassment. "Just caught up in the moment I guess."

He swallowed. “If you don’t feel like going to those kinds of restaurants, then we won’t.” Siris was looking down.

“Maybe every other day. That way we both get our way.” I sat down on the edge of my bed and looked up at Siris who was now sitting on one of the chairs flanking the fireplace across from my bed and me at the moment.

He ran his hand through his hair before he nodded. "That sounds like a plan." He looked up at me. Concerned. "How you feeling?"

Nodding, I stretched and his eyes took on a strange look before he looked away. "Much better than I've been for a while. I think I really needed that nap."

I saw him smile as he stood up and came over to me. He offered me a hand. "I'm glad. Shall we eat out on the patio?"

A smile slipped onto my lips as I slid my hand into his. "That sounds nice."

He pulled me up with a bit of a chuckle. "I had thought it was and you could watch the sunset with me. I also asked Jilliann to make another pitcher of one of her drinks for the hot tub again later so we can unwind some."

I pouted. "But I don't have another swimsuit."

He smiled as he released my hand and picked up the tray. "You have about seven now to choose from." A frown now appeared on my face and Siris chuckled. "All I asked was for a few and Jilliann's lovely daughter kind of went overboard a little. And that's with just a camera phone picture of you."

I stopped just outside the double french doors and placed my hands on my hips. "And when did you take that picture?"

He beamed like a little kid after he set the tray on the beautiful dinette set that was almost against the stone railing. "It was one of the times you thought I was texting someone which I was but sending Jilliann's daughter your picture too."

"You sneaky."

He laughed as I came over and sat down. Siris looked very proud and happy about how he got to take my picture while I was none-the-wiser. "Thank you so much for that compliment."

I was startled and I managed to keep it inward when strong hands slipped onto my shoulder and slid down the length of my arms. "Just remember my mortal, you are tied to me and are mine. I will not share you with any mortal. When you are alone again, I'll show you just how tied to me you are." Horus whispered so seductively sending shivers down my whole body. Goosebumps crawled along my skin at his words.

My eyes lifted up to Siris and he didn't see anything as he was finishing placing the places in front of our seats and the two drinks in front of us before taking his seat. He lifted his glass to me and I did the same. "To the beginning of our working relationship." I mirrored his statement and we clinked out glasses together before taking a sip.

Dinner was very nice especially with the sunset. Horus had misted away as he did at times after he again sent shivers to race through my body. All he did was breathed a breathe on my neck and and said just one word. "Later."

After dinner, Siris smiled as he showed me the swim suits that apparently Jilliann had washed already and placed in one of the many unused draws in the massive walk-in closet. And every one of them were beautiful.

"So...which one are you going to wear first?"

I blushed seeing him leaning against the door frame of the closet. "They're all so pretty that I don't think I can decide." I had spoken down to the seven little things laying so neatly that I hadn't even made to touch them.

A tiny squeak slipped out of my mouth as a hand covered my eyes. Siris chuckled and I felt it on my back as he pressed up against me. His chin coming to rest on my shoulder as if we had always been like this. His other hand reached around me and going into the draw from the feeling.

There was no way to help the giggle that came out from this position. "Are you choosing for me?"

He turned his head with his chin still on my shoulder. "As you can't choose, I thought I'd help." His hand over my eyes slipped away as he held one up for me. It was a lavender bikini with antique silver printed metallic swirls over the whole fabric. There was even a few lavender beads with a thin line of the antique silver around the middle of the beads. "What do you think?"

My blush hurt as it brightened. "It's very beautiful."

He lifted his head but didn't move away. "Say you'll wear it." For yet again that night, I shivered at the sound of a man speaking seductively into my ear being so close. But this time, he felt it as the shiver raced down my body. Siris chuckled as if he did it on purpose.

I swallowed and nodded. "Thank you." My voice was breathless with the affects that I never felt from anyone else stirring within my body by two very handsome men.

He smiled. "You're welcome." Siris leaned over and placed a soft kiss on the side of my neck. He didn't realize that he just hit the one spot that made my knees weak. I was more than glad that he had a hand around my waist to hold me up from falling.

He started to kiss more and I felt my heart racing as I was becoming more aroused with his tender and seductive kisses. Little soft moans and sighs started to slip out of my mouth as I panted.

After a minute of that, Siris slowly and delicately turned my face to him and he kissed me softly, cautiously at first. My eyes having closed a long time ago in this heated moment. His hand around my waist slipped to my hip as his other that was on my cheek slipped down my neck and continued. There was a part of me that wanted him to continue.

In an instant, Siris was thrown back causing me to slump to the floor. My breathe was heavy as I turned to see Siris as he gripped the door frame. He too was having to catch his breathe.

He swallowed deeply. "I'm sorry. There's no excuse for what I just did."

"There's nothing to feel sorry for." I leaned against the drawers of the closet built-ins. "I've never had anyone kiss me like that or made me feel..." I blushed as I was about to say 'loved'.

He slid down against the door frame. "Have you never had a boyfriend?"

I shrugged looking down. "I'd never called them boyfriends as they wanted nothing more than use me as eye candy. Just a girl they could claim was theirs. I never had a say in it."

Siris frowned as he pushed his knees up and rested his forearms on them. "Every girl has a say in who they are dating."

"I didn't. Just as I never had a say in anything about my life. My own biological father wouldn't even have a conversation with me at the funeral, the only time I met him. He just took one look at me and turned away."

"I'm sorry Bea."

I shook my head looking up at him. "You're the only one throughout my whole life that has made me feel like I have a choice now. That you want to help me find out who I really want to be."

He looked down. "But I didn't give you a choice to come here. I just made the decision and whisked you away from everything you knew, your life, and brought you into mine. I feel terrible about that."

I got up and knelt down in front of him. "Thank you. Even if you had asked again, I would have said yes. I think you had already known that and did what was best for me. No one has done that before."

"But your mother..."

I shook my head. "She never treated me as hers. I was just an inconvenience that she was saddled with after a summer affair with another man while her husband was out to sea. One that knew she had cheated when she had me."

Siris took my untattooed wrist and tugged me down to sit with him. He wrapped me in his arms. "Do you want to talk about it?"

My shoulders lifted and fell in a 'I-don't-care' sort of way. "Why?"

He turned my chin up and looked intently right in my eyes. "I can see that it's eating at you from inside." His hand shifted to cup my cheek. That gesture was feeling so different now after that kiss, but still the same too. "Let me help you just by being someone you can tell anything and everything to. I want to help free you from all your pain."

His eyes looked like a thought streaked through them so fast that I could have missed it if I had blinked. "How about you change and meet me at the hot tub. I bet Jilliann has her special brew already whipped up and waiting for us to get down there."

In a blink, I was up and he was gone with the door closed behind him. All I could do was stand there for a second and stare at the mirror on the back of the door. The change his his thinking left me beyond confused. After a few minutes, I shrugged and went to get changed and go down to the hot tub.

Chapter Eight

I smiled seeing Siris leaning against the hot tub. He had a hand resting against his forehead. But I slowed my progression to him when I heard his words as if he were talking to someone that wasn't in the room with him. "I know. I've already said that I was sorry. I can't help the feelings I am having for her. She's just perfect and everything I've been looking for even before you saved my life. Please. Even with you telling me that, let me be with her."

His hand fall, but his eyes were closed. I had stopped when he said he had feelings for someone. There was a feeling that he was talking about me that squeezed at my heart. Will he still feel that way when he fully knows me? I was a little afraid that he might stop thinking I was perfect once he knows everything about me.

"Please, I beg of you to not stop us from being together again. My back still stings a little from when you throw me back. All you had to do was startle me, not hurt..."

I shyly looked down as he finally looked up at me. "Bea! I...I..."

I shook my head as I continued to walk over to him as he remained where he was. My legs were a bit shakier as I came to stand next to him. I just couldn't look up to him just yet and see the thoughts in my eyes.

His hand slipped into mine. The sound of him swallowing hard made me blush. "Ready to start relaxing even more?"

I slowly looked up at him hoping that my eyes weren't going to betray me. "Yes please."

He smiled lightly as his other hand slipped to the dainty bow that held my wrap around me. Just as his hand started to untie it, it shifted sharply away. His jaw clenched a little before he blew out a breathe and his head dropped down.

Before he could turn away, I cupped his cheek and he looked at me. "You have a God too, don't you?"

His body sagged. "You heard what I said." He glanced over to the side and smiled more to himself. "Guess my secret is out."

"Told you to step outside for a moment."

I snapped my head over to see Osiris with his arms crossed frowning. There was absolutely no way I wasn't going to slip away from Siris and run over to Osiris throwing myself into his arms. His laugh echoed off the windows and walls.

I pulled back and he smiled at me. "You are tied to Siris?"

He nodded. "But our connection is different from the one you know."

"Wait, her tattoo?"

Osiris turned to Siris and nodded. "I was surprised that you had glossed over it so quickly."

"I didn't. I am just having a hard time translating a portion of it. Those symbols are just too old." Siris crossed his arms and it looked like he was sulking.

"Would you like for me to translate for you?" Osiris took my wrist with the tattoo and turned it up.

Siris came over and placed his hand over the tattoo. I jerked my wrist out from under his hand placing it against my chest. "Please don't cover it up."

He looked at me with a frown as Osiris placed a hand on his shoulder. "She is correct to not wish another to cover it wholly with their hand. That action forces my son back to the tomb he was forced into long ago. Only with it seen can my son walk around freely." My heart clenched as I looked around. Osiris placed a hand on my shoulder. "He'd leave and return where he is if he's not with you."

I looked to him. "But I didn't like how he looked when he did come back last time." Worry thick in my voice.

Osiris pulled me back to him so he was hugging me. "He'll be fine young one. My son is strong and a warrior beyond the like in all of your history."

I looked over at Siris before looking up to Osiris again. "Why don't you let Siris and I..."

Osiris placed finger over my lip stopping me. "I have my reasons and one being my son. He isn't one to let another touch what he has laid claim to." He chuckled when I looked at him confused. In response, he lifted my wrist up a bit more. "This ties you to my son. He recreated something very close to what was placed on him and Bastet."

My hands weakly gripped Osiris' robes as I felt the world swim around me. A part of me pulled me from reality. Siris moving to catch me with Osiris. Osiris telling both of us that I will be alright in a moment. Telling me to embrace what I see and learn.

~*~*~

Taking a deep breathe to calm my nerves, I raised my chin as I walked in with my father by my side. I knew he didn't want me to tie myself to Horus, but he couldn't deny how much more alive I've been with him in my life. My father had always wanted me to find someone and I never understood why he didn't want me to be with Horus.

Up front next to the alter stood Horus and his father. Both smiling, but Horus looked in a daze at seeing me in all my ethereal glory. I was wearing what only the other Gods would ever see adorn on my body. This was an important day and I wanted Horus to know how happy I was to tie myself to him.

I took my place on the other side of the alter facing Horus. His father turned to him looking very proud. "Do you come into this fully willing and not against your true will?"

Horus smiled more. "This is what I wish."

My father turned to me. "And do you come into this fully willing and not against your own true will?"

I smiled more right back at Horus. "This is what I wish."

Both our fathers nodded in unison. They each guided us to stretch out our hands to the other across the alter slab. Horus took my hands and wrapped his hands around my wrists. I followed doing the same.

I felt our fathers switche places before I felt the soothing touch of Osiris. He placed his hand over the small of my back. I knew my father was doing the same to Horus. This was something we'd do together as it always should be.

Slowly our fathers started chanting and their voices drifted together. But just as their voices brought an unearthly beautiful sound, it also brought on a pain. A pain that I mortal would never be able to bare a second of. Both Horus and I gripped each other to bare this pain. He was my sturdy ground in which I could bare anything.

Our fathers moved and their hands glided over our backs and down our arms. In their wake was a soul tingling feeling along with the pain. When they got down to our hands, my father's hand was over one set of hands and Osiris was over the other set. They held tight as their voices grew and the pain increased in such a small part of our bodies.

As the last of their chanting turned to a deep hum, the pain changed to an awareness. The feel of the hands in mine with the heart beat of the man that I felt completely. My fingers spread across his wrist as I felt him do the same.

We seemed to lift our heads up at the same time. There was this pull now as I looked into Horus' eyes. He tugged me onto the alter. When I was kneeling on the alter, Horus rose himself up onto it too. He cupped my cheek pulling me so close our hearts beat together as one through our skin. As if we couldn't stop ourselves, we kissed deeply.

We only kissed for a few minutes before we pulled away and smiled. My eyes caught the fading symbols that bound Horus to me and I knew mine were doing the same. Only another god will see the mark that shall remain on our backs where our fathers had started.

~*~*~

My eyes fluttered open and I groaned at the dizzy feeling that made me feel so weak. There was a wet cloth on my forehead which moved away and was placed back on my forehead feeling cooler than it left. The hand that had replaced the cloth skimmed down my cheek gently.

I looked up to find Siris seating on the edge of one of the lounge chairs next to me. He smiled, but not fully. I knew he was concerned over me again. "How do you feel?" His words were soft and soothing.

Nodding, I started to sit up and he had helped me because I felt very weak. After I was up, we sat there looking into each other's eyes. My chest against his front. His arms wrapped around my petite body being my support. "I'm feeling much better now. Thank you."

He smiled more as he moved one of his hands to remove the cloth that now rested against my shoulder. He placed it on the seat next to us. "You still up for relaxing in the hot tub?"

I smiled too. "What are we waiting for?"

He laughed and in a heart beat I yelped as he scooped me up taking me over to the hot tub. I was all too happy to find myself in his arms so I didn't have to walk right now. This time his hand wasn't moved away when he untied my wrap dress and he helped me out of it.

He held two glasses of Jilliann's concoction in his hands as he returned to the hot tub. Once in, he glided over to me and handed me one of the glasses. "The doctor called me earlier and told me you can have as much alcohol as you want. That his tests showed that you've healed just enough that you didn't worry about drinking. So..." He smiled as he lifted up his glass. "I would be remiss in not sharing half the pitcher with you. I have to maintain my gentlemanly status."

I giggled as I took a sip of the drink. The drink was sweet and a little sour but in the good way. I licked my lips before I took another drink. Siris chuckled as he sat across from me drinking his own.

After three glasses, it was safe to say I was nicely tipsy. Siris at the moment held me with my back against his front. His hands working my shoulders to loosen those tight muscles.

"Would Osiris be mad if we did try?" I laid my head on Siris' shoulder.

He smiled kissing my nose. "He promised not to get involved again. If we choose to try, then he will stay out of it. He disapproves, but he will not stop anyone from trying to be happy."

I shifted and turned around on his lap smiling. My legs went around his hips so I was straddling him. His hands having slipped down to my own hips. "So we could?"

In my mind, I thought Siris would have been happy, but he frowned. "I think we should just go slow. Things are a little... complicated."

When I started to look down, he stopped me and lifted my chin up. "I'm not saying no, just go easy. I want to show you how much you have come to mean to me."

I pouted tracing little circles on his bare chest just at the water line. The bubbles having been off for a little bit now. "Does that mean no kissing?"

Siris laughed. "You like how I kiss." He smiled proudly as he leaned forward. I half thought he was about to kiss me, but he just rested his forehead against mine. "I like how you kiss too. I've never had anyone make me feel like that through a kiss as you had made me."

"I've never had anyone care about me the way you do."

Siris pulled me closer to him and he laid my head on his shoulder. "Then everyone you've known have been blind."

I started to relax against him and he held me tight. "It's alright to go to sleep. In a little, I'll take us to our beds." His voice whispering into my ear with his cheek against my own. He started humming and he lulled me off to sleep right there against him.

~~~

A soft moan drifted out of my mouth as I felt a hand cup one of my breasts. The feeling of tingles were pulling me out of my sleep. Lips graced my skin that was exposed at the top of my breast from my outfit. These feelings were doing more to me both physically and emotionally than I've ever felt before.

I opened my eyes to see Horus as he was looking up at me. He growled and I gasped as it made me feel instantly aroused. "I promised I'd show you that you're mine and that no mortal can do what I can. You will feel my claim on you before I'm through with you."

All I could do was gasp when he moved my bikini top that was still on me to the side and he breathed over my exposed sensitive nipple. He grinned before he swirled the tiny bud with his tongue and then he wrapped his lips around it. My back arching as he kissed my little nipple squeezing my breast gently with his hand.

His free hand slipped down my body, over my hip, and around my thigh. My breathe caught as his fingers touched me against my most
~~~

private area. The bikini bottom providing the only barrier between his tingling touch and me. My legs spreading for him to give him access to my moist and wanton self. My body having a mind of its own. He seemed to enjoy what he was doing to me.

He shifted over to the other breast as his free hand skimmed the edge of the bikini bottom while he went toward the bow that held the bottom together. I felt his fingers as he slowly untied the bow. He made sure I felt what he was doing. The feeling was so amazingly sensual that it made me so very close to begging him to take me.

His mouth moved away from my nipples and started to ascend as his tingling touch slipped back between my legs where he moved the fabric aside and touched me truly. I couldn't decide which would grab my attention more. The way he kissed, sucked, and nipped at my skin as he went up my neck. How his fingers held magic as he rubbed and teased me like no one had ever done before. And teasing was what it was more like. Making me want more, so much more. I was nearly shaking with my want.

A soft intake of air came from me when he nipped my earlobe. His finger dipping in for a second before he continued to tease me. His heated breathe fanned against my neck. "Tell me what you want my mortal." His voice so deep that it touched my soul and increased my wantonness.

"Please." I gasped softly when he dipped his finger in more into my slick self. He was being such a tease and he knew it. He reveled in it with great pleasure. He wanted me to want him desperately.

I felt his smile as he slowly tortured me. "Please what?" He rubbed his lips down and up the column of my neck. "You must tell me so I may do what you wish."

I took his wrist when he was about to remove it again. "Please. More. I need more."

He chuckled as he did as I asked and moved his finger within me skillfully. After a moment he added another finger while his lips kissed a part of my neck. I moaned when he sucked hard on that spot taking me higher. My hips moved with his hands' movements and my breathing had accelerated as my heart pounded with desire.

After he was satisfied with the spot he most likely placed a mark on was well marked, he slowly and painfully descended down my body just as I felt myself peaking. Once he kissed the junction between my hip and my lower stomach, I climaxed. He was just so skilled that he made it last several minutes.

The moment my climax settled down, Horus grinned boldly and leaned down. He dragged his tongue from back to front between my legs. I gripped the sheets as the sensation was more than what his fingers made me feel. My back aching too as he concentrated and lavished my womanhood better than anyone who bothered to do that for me.

He pulled not one, but two climaxes out of me before he released my hips that he had held down while he went down on me. As I caught my breathe after the second one, he rose up and looked down at me. "Have any mortal made you feel like that?"

I shook my head feeling very shaky. "No."

He smiled. "Is it your wish that I show you more?"

"How could there be more?" My mind couldn't even make a thought let alone think of what else he could do to please me. What he just did as most likely left me reeling for hours if not days. And I didn't want to have this sensation to dissipate anytime soon.

He looked deep into my eyes. "If you have my beloved's memories, then you know what more I can do privately to the one that is tied to me."

A deep blushed flooded my cheeks as her memories came to my mind. "We don't have to do that." Even though I said that, I desperately wanted to experience first hand what those memories held.

His eyes darkened as his hands throw my legs around his waist. "But your eyes tell me you wish to. Tell me the truth my beautiful mortal. You wish for me to slip into you and take you to the brink and back again and again and again."

In a swift movement I nearly missed, he stripped off his cloth that he wore so he was now completely bare. As everything else he did so far, he went slowly as he entered me. I felt every inch of him within me. He was so perfectly sized that he filled every millimeter of my slick passage with his mighty self.

Horus took his time as he pulled climax after climax out from within me. Even when he flipped me around so quickly and took me from behind did he have me at his slow mercy. When I started to get weak from his mastery, he held me up with an arm around my waist.

His hand covered my mouth as I hit my ultimate peak and he stiffened. He had come too. His voice being able to give sound when I shouldn't or someone would come running. More likely it would have been Siris and this wouldn't be a position I'd want him to see me in. Not after that kiss we shared together in my closet.

Horus released me and I laid down flat on my stomach feeling completely sated and spent. My eyes closing as I drifted into a complete sleep. I felt Horus lean down and kissed a sore part of my neck. "You are mine above all others." His words followed me as I dreamt for the rest of the night.

Chapter Nine

I woke the next morning and blushed. Horus was laying next to me looking totally at peace. From what I could see, he was completely bare still and was showing everything if my shoulder wasn't blocking the view of his... ahem... Godhood. My eyes traveled up to his face and he was completely asleep. This was the first time I've ever seen him asleep and totally relaxed besides when he's being his cocky, arrogant God self.

Even seeing his God face, it didn't affect how I saw him. He looked...sweet in this one moment. Maybe it's the euphoria of what happened in the middle of the night, or just seeing him like this that's making me feel this way. I was softening more with him.

With a sigh, I started to wiggle out of his hold. Alas, I got an inch away before Horus shifted his body and then I was pinned. His very large muscles of his arms wrapped around my chest and his head in the croak of my neck. His breathe doing tricks against my skin.

"You will not leave just yet my mortal." His voice smiled at me and not at all filled with any sleep.

"But the day is starting. I have to get up."

He shook his head and my cheek was caressed by his silky soft feathers that changed as he shook his head. A part of me frowned loving the feel. I did when he rose up and looked down at me with his gorgeous eyes. "I will keep you trapped just a little longer."

Another sigh, I gave in. "How can I fight you?"

He smirked his most cocky smile. "You could never. I'm a God after all."

I smiled at him. "One who's very full of himself."

He laughed as the side of his hands slid down my sides sending my lower stomach all a flutter with desire again. Horus lowered his head back to my ear. "If I remember correctly, you were so full of myself last night." I gasped as his hands spread my legs and placed them around his waist. "And you could be again right now."

My face went scarlet as I smacked his hands off my legs. "Not now. I'm still very sore from you last night and will need to get ready to leave with Siris."

An ache started in my heart thinking of Siris. After what Horus has done, where would Siris stand now? I didn't want to reject him because I cared for him too. A great deal at that. But I also didn't want to string him along because I'm starting to fall for Horus. I didn't want to hurt him.

Horus had seen the change in me and tilted his head as he looked down at me again. "What's wrong my sweet mortal?"

I shook my head. "Nothing. I'm just having one of those silly mortal woman moments."

He frowned as he stroked my hair. "Tell me. I'll help to make you better."

Again I shook my head. "You wouldn't understand."

"After what we have, I believe I could understand anything you're feeling." He shifted as he wasn't fully over me. His hawk face that had returned when he was asleep fading into his handsome face.

"Can I just get up please? I think I just need to shower and just start the day."

Though reluctant, Horus nodded and helped me up. He tried to enter the shower with me, but I begged him for a little peace right now. He asked again what was wrong but I couldn't tell him.

There was no way I could tell him that I was in love with both him and the man who took me in. Both have cared for me, and I had fallen for both. I didn't know which I loved more at the moment and don't know if I will ever love one more than the other.

In the shower, I let the water beat heavily on my back. My muscles relaxing from the workout Horus had put me through the night before. I would still have a bit of a limp for the rest of the day because of him. Right now I was letting my now very complicated life slip away in loo of giving myself this time before I had to head back to reality.

~~~
~~~

The smiled that lit Siris' face twisted my heart a little bit more. But still, I returned his smile happily as I took a seat at the breakfast table in his gorgeous kitchen. Guilt tugging at me for not knowing what I was supposed to feel for either my God or the man that had my heart warring with itself for whom it wanted.

"Did you sleep well?" His hand sliding into mine as he always did every morning. Though the more gentle feel of his hand that held mine had more meaning now. That too made my guilt hit me harder.

I blushed and then proceeded to wince as I crossed my leg over the other knee. "It was...nice." What was I saying? It was more than nice. Last night was beyond anything I had ever experienced and I doubt I will ever experience for the rest of my life. For heaven sakes, a God from ancient Egypt had made love to me last night very passionately.

Siris lifted an eyebrow and I felt his hand slide just a hair out of mine. Almost as if he knew what had happened in the middle of the night. "Did he...?"

My blush deepened as Julliann set a plate for each of us on the table. I held my tongue till she left and turned to Siris. "He woke me last night while I was sleeping. I think it was because of what he was doing and the alcohol that I..." I groaned softly and cupped my face placing my elbows on the table.

How could I even tell Siris? How much will it kill him to hear this from me. But I didn't want to keep this from him. Didn't want to keep anything from him no matter how much it hurt him. He deserved every bit of truth from me.

"You what?" I could hear that his gut was twisting with pain at what I was about to say.

I couldn't look at Siris. Not with the images playing in my mind. Of Horus and the feelings that lingered in my body from his skill. "Begged for him." I dared not say it more than just loud enough to be heard.

Siris shifted closer to me and draped an arm over my shoulders pulling me toward him. Comforting me even if he was hurting. "You have nothing to be ashamed of." I looked up at him and he smiled down at me. A smiled that said he was a little hurt but that he understood. How could he compete with a God? "Do you wish to still try?" I shyly nodded laying my head on his shoulder. He gave me a light squeeze. "Then we will."

I smiled and hugged him before we broke away to eat our breakfast. I felt better telling Siris about last night. I didn't want any secrets between us ever. None at all now that both our secrets were out in the open.

~~~

A giggle slipped out as Siris slipped under the surface of the hot tub. It was a complete accident, and we were both very tipsy from this latest creation of Julliann's. I've only had one glass and he's had two. We really shouldn't be this tipsy, but we were.

He sputtered as he surfaced after sliding off his seat. Spitting out the very warm water with a smirk. "Guess Julliann wants us drunk tonight."

I nodded. "It seems that way and now I get to see her drinks affect you." He grinned and took another sip of his drink and I mimicked him.

It's been two weeks now since we decided to see how things developed. Only a few times has he managed to break the agreement we made about lunch. Each time it was to a very, very fancy restaurant. You know the ones where each plate cost about a hundred dollars per person. He'd even get me to dress up to go to the restaurant.

I didn't mind now as I was used to those little moments he'd lavish me with something. He doesn't do it too often which was nice. Only four times in the last two weeks. For him, that was very good use of restraint.

Siris smiled as he glided over to me. His hands going to the ledge on either side of me. His knees resting on the floor of the hot tub. My arms were resting on the lower ledge just under the surface of the water.

"So my sweet Bea... We're all alone and if we have all that concoction in the pitcher, we'll be drunk. Have you ever been drunk before?"

Another giggle. "Once." I managed to hide the cringe tat laid behind that one little word.

"Hmm..." He leaned forward. "Do you want to again?"
~~~

Sliding my hands over the edge of the water and around his neck. "Do you?"

Smirking, he wrapped his hands around my waist. "I don't think we really need to." He gave me a short kiss. "I think the drink we have already had is working just fine." He kissed me more and I was completely his in that moment.

I arched into him as he skimmed my lower lip asking for entrance which I gladly gave. His hands pulled me to him and I felt how much he was turned on. He was straining against his swim trunks.

My legs moved away from him and he slipped closer to me as he leaned me back against the edge of the hot tub. His tongue dominating mine and sending tingles down my spine. My heart racing as I got dizzy with desire for him.

When he pulled away and started kissing down my neck, I was completely breathless. "Am I going too fast?" I shook my head before I groaned and let my head fall back. His lips descending down my collarbone and down the center of my chest as he lifted me out of the water ever as slowly.

His hand brushed the edge of my bikini top lightly before he moved it aside painfully slow. When the fabric was aside, he dragged his lips across my skin to my tight bud where he wrapped his lips around it. I ached more as he caressed the bud with his tongue before he sucked.

Siris' hands switched and he moved the fabric away from my other breast too. His hand going to cup the now expose breast. His actions were setting my body on fire. I had no idea he could be so talented, but I shouldn't have been with everything he's told me about his past. Just as skilled at seduction as Horus, a god.

He had me in a sweet haze that when he slipped the tie of my bikini bottom undone, I was ready to shift him so he sat and I slipped over him. A swift spark of courage, and I did just that. Siris was breathing heavy too as he looked deep into my eyes while I dragged his swim trunks to his knees. His hands going to my hips to help guide me over him when I straddled him.

Both of us moaning as I lowered down upon him. Our first time being so intimate. We had been taking time and in this one moment, this was right. Us being together felt right. Us no longer dancing around this moment any longer.

But being with Horus had been right too.

I closed my eyes once I was fully seated over him. He was just as thick and long as Horus. The feel of one felt so much like the other. Both singing and resounding the same within my heart. I doubt I could ever choose between them if I had to.

Siris placed a wet hand from the water around the back of my neck. He pulled my lips back to his and started to adore me sweetly and passionately. As we made love with our lips, I started to moved over him with him moving along with me.

This wasn't like with Horus. This was what made Siris that much more different. He was gentle and caring. He'd want to show just how much he cared for me in every touch. Even like this, he was beyond passionate.

I didn't care that I was in love with two men. Not in the euphoria that I was in at the moment. And I did love both beyond reasoning. I was torn, yet right now I could care less as I felt beyond loved by Siris.

Siris' lips left mine as his lips nipped at my neck. My hands rested on the edge of the hot tub behind him. I've heard about people having sex in hot tubs before, but I had never pictured I would ever experience. Now that I was, I couldn't not help loving it as much as I loved Siris.

His hand slipped around my back and I bent backwards for his lips to continue their journey. He supported me and I felt his nimble fingers untying my top fully. Then it was flung away from the hot tub to land somewhere else. I didn't care at the moment. Not with the skilled care Siris was showering me with.

Slowly I felt Siris slid us to the other side of the hot tub. The water moved passed as he guided me backwards till I was sitting on his knees. His shins which now rested against the seat below me. He took over the rhythm of our lovemaking. My back draping over the edge as now I was only partially submerged.

My hands returned to a ledge, but this time it was to either side of me. Just like with Horus, all I could do was lean back and enjoy every tantalizing touch and thrust coming from the man making love to me.

Unlike with Horus, Siris never took me from behind. He seemed to prefer to stare right into my eyes as he loved me. I loved doing it like this too. To see every flutter of ecstasy and pleasure along with love that laid deep into his eyes as we found physical release of all our emotions.

~~~

We laid on a lounge chair with just a beach towel draped over us. My body laid stretched across his side. His fingers slipping in and out between my own. My hand laying lovingly on his chest. His palm gracing the back of my hand. All the time he was sending tingles across my skin.

His chest rose high as he took a deep breathe. “I'll miss this.” He said it so softly as if he wished not to speak it out loud, but that he had to just say it. As if it pained him to keep himself from voicing his thoughts.

I looked at him puzzled. “What do you mean?”

He frowned. “One reason Osiris didn't want us together because he knows that one day soon, it'll end.” His hand stopped slipping and his fingers curled under my hand to my palm. "I don't want it to end." Then his hand started again.

Looking at him, I lifted up pulling the towel with me. To keep me covered though he's seen me completely bare. I just felt a bit self-conscious after having sex. “What do you mean it'll end?”

Siris took my hand and kissed my palm. “I didn't know till he told me that night you found out about him.” He looked into my eyes and he looked so sad. “I think I should tell you how I became tied to him so you may understand more about everything.”

He shifted us so I was laying down again but on my back and he was on his side. His fingers caressing my cheek before they skimmed down my arm. His eyes following the motion. I knew he was collecting his thoughts and figuring out where he was going to start.

“I had been the typical party, get-into-tons-of-trouble-and-anything-rebellious type of rich boy growing up. I wasn't this responsible man you see today. I cared about nothing but myself. Even getting high for pleasure." He shrugged. "Back then I didn't have anything to ground me.

“What changed me was the night I was originally supposed to die.” I frowned and he smirked a little because I frowned. “I had been racing
~~~

this guy through the mountains in West Virginia. I took a turn too wide and skidded into a guard rail before my car flipped over the railing going down the cliff side a hundred feet below. Everything happened so quick and there was barely anyone around me to see it happen.

"Death didn't come quickly for me. I laid there tangled among the crumpled mess of my car praying to anyone and anything to save me. In that moment, I was a believer that there was something or someone greater out there looking out for us. I just didn't know who it was. The alcohol that had been in my system during the whole race had leaked out with most of my blood.

"It was in the moment just before my death that everything stopped. The smoke and dust stopped swirling. The pain in my body fading for a bit. That's when Osiris came to me and offered me a way to live again. In that moment between moments. All I needed to do was listen to him and allow him the use of my physical body when he is of need of it. To be tied to him."

Siris smiled as he laid his head down on my chest. My eyes fluttered close stroking his hair letting him continue on with his story. The feeling of being so comfortable and connected with him was wonderful.

"He told me how only some Gods still walk the earth plane. How Ra had made new rules for the rest of the Gods with the changing times. With so little believing in them and worshipping the new religions, followers were few and far between. As Osiris was the God of the underworld, he was told not to leave as it was his charge to look after souls. To only return when a soul that believes is about to pass on to his realm.

"But Osiris found a loop hole to that rule, me. If he made a special pact with one that was near death and I allowed myself to be tied to him, he's able to leave the underworld for short periods of time before he had to return. If he was inside me, it was longer."

Siris looked up at me. "You had somehow seen that he was inside me that one time before you went completely asleep. He's puzzled over that but never said anything to me. He rarely uses my body. The most he's ever used it was where you were concerned."

"Why does he care about me so much?"

He smiled as he cupped my cheek and lifted his lips to me. Kissing me ever so briefly making me feel his love. “Because he had kept your soul close to his heart for centuries before allowing you to return to a new life.” He looked into my eyes. “He wouldn’t tell me why he had kept your soul for so long, but I’ve glimpse only how protective of you he is all the time.”

“He said he couldn’t find me till we met.”

Siris nodded. “He had been distraught for years looking for you. He needed my help and that’s why he came to me for the deal. Even then, you were lost in the world till that one fateful moment.” He smiled. “I’d never forget how I felt the instant I saw you. For the half a second I got to see you that first moment before Osiris took over, I was in awe.”

I blushed as his most wanton member sprang to life and Siris chuckled. “I can’t help how perfect you looked and how even more perfect you have turned out to be. I couldn’t help falling in love with you.”

My blush grew. “Then make love to me again and show me how much you’ve fallen.”

He smiled as he leaned closer and capturing my lips as he repositioned us. He showed me just how much he loved me and it was beyond perfect. His gentleness and caring touched a part of my soul that was just for him. That not even Horus could touch no matter how he tried. But Horus had his own area too that Siris couldn’t touch.

~~Julliann’s Point Of View~~

I smiled turning back around. He tried to fool all of us with how much he liked her, but I knew they loved each other. And I was glad they were admitting their love to the other. Maybe now he’d marry and have children. A little of that concoction of mine would do it every time.

Now they were in the pool room making love to each other. Guess they didn't need me to tell them I was off or about the midnight snack. They'll find it if they needed it after they finished.

Chapter Ten

~~Bea's Point Of View~~

These past two months have been like a dream. Siris and I haven't taken our relationship any farther. We've just remained as a secret couple. Not even his students have any idea that we were together.

Horus has been a little testy since he found out. But after I told him about my feelings, he understood. I was mortal after all and my heart could be torn between two. Though he was upset that he didn't hold more room in my heart than a mortal, he still understood. He may not like it wholly, but that was how things were.

Some nights when Siris and I don't make love, Horus seduces me toward his love. I doubt I've had a night without sex with at least one of them. Both calling to a different part within me where their love resided. Both making it that much harder to tell whom I loved more and whom I could live without. Right now, I couldn't live without either and neither wanted me to chose just yet before I was certain.

A giggle slipped out as Siris leaned over the back of my computer chair and placed his hands on either side of my desk in his office. An office that was completely organized and orderly now. Books ordered by subject and then by title. Files in their right places for once ever. Artifacts catalogued and on display with their location either in the office or in other places.

"So... Do we have one of our lunch dates today?"

I pouted at him. "Haven't we ran out of places by now?"

He beamed so happily as he shook his head. "Not yet. I'm keeping the best for last." He lifted up his eyebrow. "So..."

I shrugged. "We did agree on that."

He laughed as he went over to his desk. “How about we leave in...” He looked at his wrist watch. “Twenty minutes?”

I laughed lightly. “Sure. I’ll finish up the last of this and we’ll head out for food.”

There was a knock and Siris went to answer the door so I could finish the last of these emails to students about their current grades. It was something I had started doing for them after I talked to Siris about it. He was all for it as it was one last thing he didn't have to worry about, and something that he like seeing me so happy to do.

“Ah Mr. President, welcome to my office. Can I help you with anything?”

“So I see that you do have an assistant. You forgot to inform me and I didn’t see any record of her paperwork in our system.”

My hands stilled on the keyboard for the last email as I clearly remember filling out the paperwork with Siris. We even set up an account for me were my paycheck go every two weeks. As I live with him, I have whittled him in only giving me about three bucks more than my previous job. I didn’t care about money as he preferred to pay for everything anyways. The money he put into that account was really my savings now. The card’s in my wallet, but I’ve touched it only once since I got it.

“That’s because she’s my personal assistant and not paid by the university. I have all the right paperwork in order.” Siris sounded a bit off. Like he was upset that the President of the University had looked into me.

I finished the last email and rose up. What happened next felt like time slowed as I turned to face the President of the University. But he wasn’t just the president. No, that wouldn’t have told me why he looked into me. There was a different reason.

My heart constricted in my chest as I came face to face with the man who outright rejected me. The man who with one look, turned away and whom I never saw again till this very moment. The man who I had wished before then to have known just for a moment. Just to have the smallest contact with. To tell him how much he meant to me even if I didn't know him at all.

His eyes flared as he seemed to puff up. Hate dripping from his entire body. “So my secretary was right. You have become his assistant.” His words dripped with disgust that stabbed me right through my heart.

Siris snapped his head between my own biological father and me before settling on the man, to Siris' knowledge, had no reason to hate me with a passion and fire more heated than molten lava. “Sir...” Siris had no idea what was going on. "Do you know Bea?"

"Yes." My father hissed as a sneer.

"How? When?"

My stomach twisted and I felt sick in that one moment more than I had when I had first seen that look on his face. But my father didn't bother acknowledging Siris as he marched over to me and gripped my upper arms painfully. But that didn't matter because of the hate and disgust dripping off my father's entire person and inked into my skin as a poison.

“I wouldn't give you a job and now I found you here in my university.” He pushed me back and I stumbled before clenching my desk to keep me up. "As the assistant to one of my best professors."

Tears brimming my eyes and my breathe grew choppy against the sobs deep in my chest. “That was years ago. I asked then because I had no one to turn to.” A few tears escaped as I looked up to him. “I thought you'd have a bit of mercy on me.”

“Mercy?! After what I found out about you from your boss. You have got to be delusional! Why would I ever give you a job here among good, honest people with the likes of you?”

I cupped my hand over my mouth as the first sob slipped out. What had my evil boss told my own father about me? How fucked up was he to do that to me?

There was no point in staying in front of my father any longer. I couldn't with how he made me sound. It hurt more than anything hearing those words from him. Why couldn't my family show just an ounce of love for me? What was so wrong with me that they couldn't?

Siris' voice shouted after me as I rushed out of his office. The joy of my life with him was now overshadowed by my father. He'd most likely poison Siris against me.

I bumped into people and sobbed out an apology after apology before I could push my way to the girls bathroom. Inside, I fell sick into one of the toilets. The contents of my stomach filling the bowl before I finished and flushed. Then I just knelt there sobbing and letting my tears fall into the clean toilet water.

A soft knock came to the stall door. "Bea?" I sniffed a few times as I looked to the door hearing one of Siris's Honor student's voice, Cilla. "What's wrong? Maybe I can help."

I took a deep and shaky breathe before my legs trembled as I lifted up from the floor. "I-I'm fine." I spoke to the door because I couldn't open it with how I looked at the moment. The little bit of make-up I did have on was most likely falling off with my tears. My chest was more than tight and I felt weak.

"You don't sound fine. Please open the door and we'll just talk." Cilla's voice held deep concern. After a few months of helping Siris, I've become very close with all his honor students as well as his more enthusiastic students who really wanted to know more about the subject they were studying.

My breathes were even worse as I opened the door and she saw the tears rolling down my face. Not just tears, but snot too. I was not at all a pretty sight. Not with seeing pure hate for the first time in my life.

Her face turned horrified as she looked at me. Then her features softened. "Come on." She took my hand and pulled me over to one of the leather covered benches next to the wall leading out of the bathroom. We sat down and she pulled out some tissues offering me them.

"Why does the universe hate me?" I sobbed into the tissues as I tried wiping the tears away only to have them be replaced just as quickly.

Cilla frowned. "The universe doesn't hate you. Why would you think that?" She tried to help with my tears but she was having difficulty too.

"Everything was going right for me. I have a job I love." I gave her a small smile which she returned. "Siris is the nicest boss I ever had. I didn't have to struggle for everything. These past three months have been the best of my life."

She nodded. “But something must have gone wrong for you to think the universe hates you.”

I nodded back. “My father showed up.” I bent over my lap and pressed the tissues that were in my hand to my eyes as the tears had renewed themselves.

Cilla let me cry myself out again. But that was wrong as another wave of nausea hit me and I sprinted to the toilet again. She held my hair back as I dry heaved over the bowl. Nothing was coming out as the first time had cleared me out.

When I was done, I leaned weakly against the walls to the toilet stall. Cilla put her wrist on my forehead before switching to her wrist. “You’re like ice.” Her palms went to my cheeks as my body sagged and I passed out. Everything going black into a complete nothingness.

~~~

Beep.

Beep.

I tried to groan at that sound, but nothing came out. I was in the hospital yet again. The worst place ever for me and I was here hooked up to more machines that I could feel around me. That small tube in my nose that always felt wrong but necessary.

The squeak of a door came and I thought about how painful that sound was. There was someone who was holding my hand and they shifted toward the door. From the feel, I knew it was Siris. My heart felt happy to know that Siris was here with me though he too hates hospitals ever since his death the fist time. He cared about me a lot and was glad that he was sticking by me.

"What are you doing here? Haven't you done enough?" Siris spoke though gritted teeth.

A sigh came out as the newcomer closed the door. "I just wanted to see how she was. How could I have known she was in a delicate condition?"

"She didn't know. Neither of us knew! That doesn't absolve you of what you did to her. You don't even know the first thing about Bea and yet you spouted things like that at her. What would give you the right at all?"
~~~

Another sigh. "You should sit down." My father sounded reluctant yet very determined.

"I'll stand." Siris was so pissed at his boss.

"Alright." The groan of a chair came to me before I felt my other hand being held by my father. It was odd having my father show affection after what he had said. Even his touch was strange and made me feel as if he could hold the sun in his hands.

"You might not know this, but Bea's mother named me as her biological father." I couldn't tell by the sound of his voice what he thought or felt about that.

"What..?!" Disbelief tinged with anger.

"Let me continue before you start questioning me."

Now Siris took his seat and cocooned my hand in both of his. "Go on then."

"It is true that I had a whirlwind love affair with her mother for one summer. I was young and so naive at the time. She was so beautiful and full of life. But when the summer ended, she told me she was married and went back to her husband. I had been crushed.

"A year later, I found my wife and we were very happy. Years down the road, this lawyer in a business suit shows up on my doorstep out of the blue. He proceeds to tell me that I had a child and her mother just died. He said it right in front of my wife and made it sound like I had an affair on her. For all I knew, that's exactly what she thought.

"We showed up to the funeral and she sees that Bea was too old for there to have been an affair. My wife had apologized at the time, but the damage had been done. I had been too upset to think clearly and told everyone she wasn't my daughter. Everyone believed me even if there was a seed of doubt in my mind seeing her next to that man that had been there while she grew up."

"Then why did you..."

"I'm getting to that." My father cut Siris off before he could finish his thought out loud.

A sigh. "Though it was done, I still kept the picture the lawyer gave me of Bea. It's been hidden in my desk all these years at the university.

Every now and then I had taken it out and looked at it till Bea called my house one day.

"My wife had talked to her for a good hour. When I got home, my wife handed the phone over to me telling me to talk to her. My wife looked upset so I did. Bea was begging me to help her get out of the job she had found to support herself. She wanted something even if it was to pick up trash. Anything at all."

The pause he took was a long one. It was as if my father was heart broken with his memories of our one and only real talk. "I had hung up the phone wanting to help her. But that turned when I talked with her boss. His words poisoned my heart against her. I thought the ultimate worse of Bea.

"When I talked to her next, I was so evil to her that I didn't let even her speak and defend herself. When I hung up, she was sobbing her eyes out but at that moment and every moment then on, I hadn't cared. Not till what you told me about her old boss."

"You didn't dig any farther than that, did you? Not any farther than what he said." Siris growled out finding he hated what my father had done. I doubt there was any love for my father in his heart. Not after hearing what my father said so far without hearing any more.

I felt the caress of the tips of my father's short greying beard. "No and I'll always hate myself for it. You had every right to rip me to shreds about what I didn't know about my daughter."

"You're accepting her?" I was stunned too.

Another sigh from my father. "I had the MT tell the hospital doctor that I wanted a paternity test done and I just got the results back." A hand moved my hair away from the right side of my face. "Her mother had it right. I am Bea's father by blood."

The image that came into my mind at that moment was Siris shooting up out of his seat and glaring at the older man on the other side of my hospital bed. "And you couldn't have done that when she was so young and left to fend for herself after her mother's death?"

"How could I have known? She didn't look like either of us, her mother or myself."

Siris huffed. "I could have had more time with her if you had been the father she needed. I could have met her sooner."

I felt my father stiffen. "What do you mean?" My father had heard the ominousness of Siris's statement.

I could almost feel the moment Siris ran his hands through his hair sitting back down in his seat. "About three months ago, I got some bad news from a specialist." Siris placed my hand against his cheek. "He doesn't know how much longer I've got and there's no way to save me. I'm dying."

"You should have told me. This is terrible."

"Seems like when life seems so perfect, something tarnishes it a little." His lips kissed my palm.

"You're in love with her."

Siris nodded into my palm. "More than in love. If I could, I'd become immortal for her to guard her and protect her always."

"So it's yours?" Huh? What's Siris'?

Siris nodded. "Yeah." He laid a hand over my stomach. "Who would have thought Julliann's concoctions would lead to this? I want to be able to stay and see our joy grow up."

"Unlike what I foolishly didn't get to do." My father rested his cheek against my knuckles. "But I'll stick with them and see my grandchild grow."

I gasped arching my back. Shock hitting me hard enough to throw me into consciousness. Siris was up and held my face in his hands. Blinking past my sleep that was in my eyes, my eyes scanning around trying to focus on anything. My mind a haze of what was going on.

"Shh Bea, shh. You're alright. Just in the hospital." He grimaced. "Again."

I swallowed passed the dryness and the acid taste. "Why...?"

"Just relax and I'll tell you." When I did, he smile. "That's my girl." That just made me blush and he chuckled. "Love the color that is coming back to your face when I say that." He stroked my hair like he always does.

I frowned. "You're stalling."

He smiled. "Can't blame me for that." He adjusted and sat on the edge of my bed. "First I need to ask you how you're feeling right now. Not nauseous are you?"

I shook my head. "No. Just a bit weak and very hungry now."

He smirked. "I'll see about dinner for you in a little." His thumb rubbed soft circles on the back of my hand. "Do you remember anything that happened?"

I looked down and nodded sniffling. "The president of the university came in and he hates me." My voice lowered "Just for living."

Siris tilted my chin up so I looked at him. "Your father doesn't hate you."

Tilting my head to the side, I looked at him a little taken back. "How do you know he's my father? I don't tell anyone as he'd not want me to." I leaned into Sirs' hand as a tear trickled down. "He doesn't want me at all."

My eyes snapped over when I felt another sit on the other side of my bed. I got a little frightened seeing my father, but that diminished slightly as he held my hand. "I do want you. I just was never sure you were my daughter. Now I am and want to make up for all the pain I caused you over the years." He held my hand between both of his as he looked like he was praying. "Please forgive this old fool."

I looked to Siris and he shrugged. "I'll sock him for you if you want."

My father raised me eyebrow at Siris. "You'd strike your boss?"

Siris shrugged to him now. "You hurt my girl, it's only fair." He then grinned. "We're also in a hospital and you could get looked at very quickly. Then you could go in tomorrow with a nice shiner."

I watched them interact and was still confused. "Um..." They both looked down at me and I frowned at them. "Will either of you tell me why I'm stuck in the hospital?"

Siris' shoulders sagged a little with his sigh. "After chewing out your father, I had ran after you. When I got to the bathroom, one of my students saw me and said that there was something wrong with you. She pulled me into the women's restroom and I saw you on the floor. Cilla was trying to get you to respond to her without success.

"When she looked up to me she was in a panic. Said that you had thrown up, cried, then tried to throw up again. After nothing came up and you sat back, she noticed how pale you got and went to check your temperature. You had grown colder and then passed out. She said your heartbeats weren't right."

He paused as he looked at my dad. "We had to call an ambulance as the university nurse took one look at you and didn't know what was wrong."

My dad looked down. "Though I didn't know you really were my daughter, I rode with you to the hospital." Still, a soft smile came to his face as he remained looking down. He was remembering something that had happened then.

"He pulled me out when I was climbing into the back of the ambulance and slammed the door in my face." Siris shook his head. "I had to drive myself here."

My dad smirked at Siris. "Your face was priceless as the ambulance moved away."

Siris chuckled. "Yeah. I was like 'what the fuck' at you for being the one to ride with her."

I frowned. "What's wrong with me though? There had to have been a reason for me passing out like I had."

Siris nodded as he turned back to me. "The stress with another condition took a toll on you."

"Condition?"

Siris nodded as he gave me a smile. "You're pregnant." His smile fell when I felt my face pale. "Bea, are you okay?"

My head moved up and down shakily in a nod fashion. My father placed his hand on Siris' shoulder. Siris looked upset by me being upset. "Give her a moment. This is a very serious subject and we need to go slow."

Both their heads snapped to the monitor next to me before looking down at me. I couldn't breathe. My father reached beside me and pushed a button as Siris was trying to easy me. "Calm down. Everything's going to be fine."

My head started to feel dizzy. My eyes started to droop as the sound of rushing around me happened. But my body didn't care what was going on. It just wanted to go back to sleep.

Chapter Eleven

A hand caressed my cheek and I knew that it was Horus. My eyes fluttered open. He looked sad but he smiled down at me anyways. "Welcome back my mortal."

"Hi." I gave him a small smile. My life may feel like it was starting to overwhelm me, but seeing Horus here with me gave me the feeling that I could take anything. Having a God tied to you would center anyone like that.

He placed his hand on my stomach. "The baby is being bad to it's mother." I frowned and he smiled up at me. "But I'll make your mother all better."

Horus moved his right hand to my sternum. Taking a deep breathe, I felt his hands warm and the warmth slipped into me. A sigh slipped out of me when I felt the energy flowed into me and I felt so much better. More refreshed.

"Better?"

I smiled at him. "Yes, thank you."

"Anything."

I closed my eyes as reality hit. "I don't know whose baby I have."

"Shh my beautiful mortal. You can't stress yourself over that detail at the moment. From what I feel in you, stress is dangerous for you and this new life." I opened my eyes and looked at him. "If you need, I'll stay close to you and forget my searching for now. Your health is my top concern at the moment."

"But you just fixed me."

Horus shook my head. "Not fully. Only for the moment." He stroked my cheek. "It's the best I can do right now as your body is changing with this child." His hand trailed down to my stomach and over the baby.

I placed my hand over my belly with his going to rest now over mine and felt tears brimming my eyes. Horus wiped one of the tears that fell. "Why the tears my beautiful mortal?"

All I could do was sniffle. "I don't want to be a terrible mom."

His features softened down to me. "You'd never be anything but a perfect mother. This child will be the most blessed child in all the world."

My eyes looked to the door when it opened. Horus looked over and frowned. My father came in with a small bear. He seemed nervous now. "I didn't know if you liked stuffed animals, but I thought that if you might need something to cuddle."

All I managed to do was burst into full blown tears. My father rushed over to me and for the first time in my life, I was held by one of my parents. My mother had never held me at all throughout all the years she was alive.

"Everything will be alright." He whispered into my ear trying to comfort me. Something else I never had from a parent at all.

I pulled back and he pulled a handkerchief out. He dabbed my tears off my cheeks. "I'm so sorry for never being there for you." My father sighed as he looked down. "There's no excuse for how I treated you."

I smiled as I pulled the bear into my arms. He had deposited it by my side when he rushed over. "This is a good start. I never had a teddy bear before."

He smiled. "Then I'm glad." My father sat back and took my hands. "Will you forgive this old man?"

I gave him a tight smile and gave his hands a tight squeeze. "You're my father. I don't need to forgive you." My hands slipped out of his and I hugged the bear again. "Do you still think I'm a bad person?"

"How could I when all Professor Denton's students found out what had gone down and what I said to you and about you? They were all adamant that you were amazing." My father smiled. "You've even organized one of my most unorganized staff members in the whole university. All his students have noticed and spoke very passionately about what you've done for him in such a short time."

I blushed. "I haven't done much."

"Oh?" My father lifted an eyebrow. "I saw his office. That's the first time I've seen it neat and tidy. Even the cleaning staff can enter and do their jobs properly. It even smells of egyptian musk incense. The atmosphere alone is more positive and I have no doubt the students benefit from a more productive instructor."

I smiled a little at a memory came to me. "Siris does seem to be more lively. He's even dragged me on stage with him and he dressed me up as an egyptian goddess." He was doing a unit on ancient gods and their different outfits. What each piece meant and why they were significant enough for the pharaoh to dress similar.

I also remember Horus' eyes as he trailed them up and down me in the whole outfit. He seemed...excited by the look. That night he had ravaged me while the whole time calling me his mortal goddess. All I could do was enjoy that moment.

My father laughed. "He's not done that before. Now that he's organized, he's able to do more for his students and hold their interest for longer. I've been told that many want to join his class for next semester." His face fell and I knew that expression.

Hugging the bear tight, I laid my chin on its head. "So you know."

He nodded. "He let it slip earlier." My father looked at me. "That was a major shock. I didn't know he had been sick as he never let on." Then he placed his hands in mine. "Know that I will be there for you when he can't. You won't ever have to suffer alone ever again. Not ever again."

I looked to the door. "Where is Siris?"

My father chuckled. "Out with a special list for you at one of his favorite restaurants. He's getting a chef friend of his to make you a very special dinner. His words were that he wasn't going to let you 'suffer' hospital food in your condition even for a moment."

I smiled. "He and I both hate hospital food." A tiny shutter ran down my spine at having to ever eat one bit of hospital food before.

"How do you feel right now? You look a lot better from earlier." My father looked over at me as he moved a wayward strand of my hair. It was the first time he had looked like my father to me. The moment was beyond perfect to finally have after all this time.

Leaning back against the pillows of the bed, I took a deep breathe. "Better. Still a bit weak and so hungry now."

He smiled and nodded. "I had a talk with your doctor after they stabilized you and we found out why you passed out. Your system isn't like everyone else's because of my side of your family. I had them add an extra nutrient in your line."

I tilted my head to the side. "Your side?"

He smiled. "I'll tell you someday when we're on better ground. For now I need to make so much up to you."

A knock pulled us from our alone time and Siris came in with a huge smile. The smells that followed him in made me ravenous. And Siris knew it as he chuckled at the look on my face. That caused a light blush to brighten on my cheeks. My blush wasn't much more than that as I was so hungry.

My father gave my hand a little squeeze before he left my room leaving Siris and I alone now. Siris brought over the portable table and set it in front of me before he sat down on the other side and started pulling things out of the bag he had brought with him. Each dish he opened made my mouth water.

"What do you think? Did I do well?"

I smiled at Siris. "You did more than well. This all looks delicious."

He handed me an actual fork. "You should start then. I don't want either of you hungry any longer."

We started eating and I felt tons better. After the first container was empty, Siris smiled as he slid another in front of me. He was still on his first.

"When will I be released?"

Siris gave me a sweet smile. "Tomorrow morning. Your doctor wants to keep you overnight to make sure you've recovered completely." I pouted and he laughed. "You won't stay alone, I'm staying with you." He smiled again and I felt my heart melt as he touched my cheek. "I want to hold you in my arms tonight."

My eyes closed as I leaned into his touch. "I'd like that very much."

Before long, our dinner was all gone and we were both laying down on my bed. Siris had to be on his back while I had my head laying on his chest. He had changed into his lounge pants in the attached bathroom. I was in a hospital gown and the blanket draped over us making me feel very secure.

Siris' hand graced my shoulder. "I want to marry you."

I looked up at him taken aback. "What?"

He smiled and dragged his knuckles lightly along my cheekbone. "I want you as my wife."

"You do?" My voice sounding insecure.

He pulled me up to him. "How could I not? Before my almost death, I had been dreaming of a woman like you. You're my perfect woman and I don't want to die without the whole world knowing that I love you with my whole soul."

My eyes went to the inside of my wrist. "But are we able to marry each other? What about our Gods?"

Horus' hand slid over his tattoo. Tingles caressed throughout my whole body. "It will change nothing between us. To the mortal world, you will be his. But in my world, you're mine. I will not stand in the way if you wish to do this."

I looked over at him strangely. Siris rubbed my back. "He's here, isn't he?"

My head nodded. "He said..." I shook my head. "I'm confused now."

"We'll talk about this another time then."

I just nodded and Siris gave me a kiss. I fell asleep with Siris holding me. The small hospital TV was on low as he liked watching the news some nights. His body heat so soothing to me helping me sleep even with the noise of the TV.

~~~

"No you don't." I yelped as Siris scooped me up into his arms and set me back down in the wheelchair. "The doctor said that you couldn't walk out of here as it was hospital policy. You should be used to this."

I pouted. "It's a terrible rule." Sulking in the wheelchair as he smirked and started us out of my room toward my freedom. It wasn't like
~~~

this was the first time we had this little exchange. Siris understood completely, but he didn't want to get into trouble with the hospital for letting me walk out of here when I didn't come in that way. You walk into the hospital, then you can leave the same way.

Out the front doors, he leaned down. "Now you can stop sulking so beautifully. My driver will be here in a moment." And on cue, his town car pulled up and stopped in front of us. "Now lets get you out of this evil chair." I giggled letting him pull me up.

I watched him push the wheelchair back inside and giggled at how he was being playful while he did. But in a moment, everything changed. The sound of screeching tires and Siris' eyes growing wide before he started running with the look of panic stretching across his face. I was frozen where I stood as the sound came from right behind me. The air blowing passed me in a mighty gust.

Hands gripped me and yanked me off my feet. My body frozen and stiff with fear. My eyes wide staring right at Siris. As darkness swallowed the edges of my view, a cloth with a sickly sweet smell hit me. They covered my mouth and nose with that cloth so I breathed in that smell all the way. I couldn't even wrap my mind around what was going on as the seconds felt like hours.

Slowly my vision hazed after the sound of a thick metal door slid and slammed shut cutting off my view of Siris. The wailing of tires under me as I was forced to sleep. My soul screaming out just wanting to just know love and nothing else. To never be taken from the ones I loved.

~~Siris' Point Of View~~

I couldn't breathe. My mind couldn't comprehend what I was seeing. I tried to force myself to move faster as the black van smoked to a stop behind my car and two men dressed in black rushed out. They grabbed Bea before I could get to her. Her eyes staying with me as they pulled her into the van. One of the men had elbowed my driver when he tried to prevent them from taking her.

My driver grabbed me as the door slammed shut between us. The van peeling out and nearly slamming into oncoming traffic who had to quickly slam on their own brakes to avoid the collision. My driver having to hold me back as my heart and soul screamed out in agony.

"BEA!!!" I tried to struggle against him with no luck. All I wanted was to go after them and get her back. I *needed* her back.

"She's gone." His voice gruff with my struggles.

My head flew back and I shouted at the top of my lungs. "NOOO!!!" I fell to my knees as my driver still held onto me.

A sob was threatening to boil out of me as I tried to breathe. But I couldn't. A part of me had been ripped away. Bea has become more to me than life. I thought seeing her unconscious in the university bathroom had almost killed me, but this was worse. So much worse.

"Sir..."

I looked to my driver. "I need her back. We were going to talk about getting married." Looking down at my hands. "She's everything to me. She's my life."

My driver's expression mirrored only a hundredth of the heartache that my soul was feeling. Then his features turned more sympathetic. "The authorities will get her back to you before you know it." A hint of doubt plagued his words and how he looked at me. As if he didn't know if I would ever get her back, but I had to. Nothing else in the world was more important.

Time went sideways for me as cops and people rushed around doing things. I felt on the outside and I was just there to see everything they were doing. My body was moving about. Talking to the police. Getting and giving information. But it wasn't me.

No. Osiris had taken over. He could see that I wasn't going to respond to anything. There was no way I would be of any use to anyone at the moment. I was just too numbed with pain to do anything.

By being inside my body, he got first hand memories of what happened. My soul screaming out which is what pulled him to me to begin with. He didn't bother coming to me outwardly. I was too useless and he knew time was of the essence before he knew fully what happened.

"You need to snap out of this, boy." Osiris was still talking to others while he was trying to get me to come back around.

"I couldn't. She's gone. Bea. My heart. My love. My life."

"She needs you to be strong. Needs you to chase after them and save her. Be the man that rescues her from her captors."

"She has your son next to her. He could save her."

"You FOOL!" My heart clenched as he forcefully showed me a still of Bea inside the van. Her eyes fearful as one of the black cladded men covered her mouth and nose with a cloth. I saw how she was in vivid clarity. He practically shoved the image into my "face" so I saw how the other guy had her. More importantly had her wrist.

"But how would they know?" My mental eyes staying on the image of the man's hand wrapped around her wrist right where the tattoo Horus had placed there. She was cut off from the only one who could save her in an instant. But he couldn't save our girl right now. They were preventing that.

"Someone has been watching and knows all about my kind."

"How can we get her back?"

"By doing what we can to locate them. I need your help though."

"My help?"

Osiris smiled internally at me as he sensed me coming back to him. *"Yes, son. You have a very deep connection with her now. Deeper than I had thought would ever develop. Your souls had bound together. She is as bound to you as she is with my son. She cannot decide between you two as you both are a part of her soul equally. This I had no idea would happen."*

My heart for some strange reason soared just then. *"She loves me?"*

Osiris' booming laugh resounded around me as I sat in the darkness of my mind and body. *"Yes boy, she loves you and you know it. Now help me and we'll be able to save your sweet beauty."*

In that moment, I made the vow to help save Bea with all my soul. Osiris thanking me but telling me something that he had kept a secret from me about Bea. I think at that moment was when I became completely Bea's and only hers. To know that and now I knew without a doubt why I had been calling her that nickname. That my own soul had a reason to give her that nickname. It had to be why fate had brought us together.

Chapter Twelve

~~Bea's Point Of View~~

My mind was hazy as I blinked awake. I coughed against the dryness of my throat. But when I went to move, I froze at the feeling of what I was wearing. Not on my full body, but around my neck. The rest of me didn't matter with that heavy weight that brought panic up inside my gut.

I reached up and touched my neck only to come into contact with something metal. A very heavy metal. My fingers tracing up and down the length of what I could only assume was a collar. It stretched from about an inch under my jaw to below my collarbone. It was loose enough for me to swallow, but there seemed to be no way it was attached to me, or how it was placed on me. No seam or break in it where it could be taken off.

That wasn't all I found. On the back, linked to a metal ring there, was a chain. Twisting around on the bed that I had been laying on, I found where the chain was sunk deep into solid concrete walls that looked thicker than I could see. There was no way to even think of breaking the chain with how thick it was.

Pulling on the chain, it just went taunt and nothing more happened. I was chained to a wall in a room that looked like it was in a bunker somewhere. Whoever had me here meant to hold me here. As if I knew where I was to begin with to even think about escape. All I knew was that my soul was screaming to get out of here and back to both my guys, Siris and Horus. All I wanted was to be held by both of them and never be let go.

Looking down at my clothes, I found I had been redressed in a very revealing outfit. One plucked right out of Egypt's greatest times. The time of the pharaohs. The top that ordained my chest was heavily beaded and only it's weight and positioning seemed the only reason my breasts remained covered. My hair was contained in a headdress like you would see in images of the pharaohs. The mirror leaning against the concrete wall showed me every detail and I looked so much like my dreams. Her memories.

I jumped when the loud groan of a thick metal door opened. My breathe sucked in as fear settled in my blood. The man smirked as he came into the room closing the thick door behind him. He moved differently now then all the years I knew him.

Maybe it was the outfit he had on. Just a loin cloth made of black fabric and embroidered with dark colors. The imagery was almost chaotic in feeling. He used to wear just tired and ill-fitting business suits. This was so different from then, yet still not at all appealing in any way.

He crept onto the bed and I tried to move away, but he was quick to catch my leg and jerk me back. "Now now. Is that any way to act when I finally have you back under me?" I felt disgusted at his implications. As if we had been lovers for the whole time I had worked for him.

I pushed at his chest furiously scowling. "Get off me." I kicked and tried so hard to knock him over.

He just laughed at my efforts. His hands holding my hips down tightly. "Not this time." He leaned down with a smirk. "This time you will be mine and no other's."

Releasing one of my hips and he gripped my forearm where the tattoo was inked. "This special leather band over your binding tattoo insures you're completely alone and all mine. He's back where he's been since her death. Where he belongs."

He grinned as my face paled. Realization hit me hard in my chest. My evil old boss knew of Horus and his story. Knew that I was tied to him. He seemed to be gloating over how Horus was once again stuck in a hell Ra had fashioned for him. "I have known since you returned early that you help that thief Horus escape from his entombment."

My eyes stayed on the band that covered my connection to Horus. The thick leather strap that was the color of half dried blood and it had lots of hieroglyphics, many more than the tying tattoo that Horus had placed on the wrist below. Each line of symbols were only half an inch wide. There were so many rows of them and some glittered in the light with an eerie shine.

My body went limp as reality set in. I was cut off from the one I knew could help me. Horus had been my secret hope when I found that I was chained to this room. But he hasn't shown up or been there at all. For the first time since he tied me to him, I was completely alone and defenseless.

"So you see, you're all mine now."

I snapped out of my stupor when I felt him clasp metal cuffs onto my wrists. In that moment, I realized what he was going to do to me. My fight came back to me as I thought of the child growing inside me. The child of one of the two men that has a piece of my heart and soul. It didn't matter whose it was at this moment. All that matter was the child I carried.

"I'll never be yours! NEVER!"

In one swift movement and with strength I didn't know was inside me or that I was capable period, I managed to somehow kick my demented old boss off me. Strength surged through me as I yanked at the cuffs binding me to a bedpost on either side of me. The metal snapped as it ripped through the wood of the bed.

A fury I never knew existed coursed through my veins. I felt the need for blood. The need to protect my child more than anything thick in my veins and hardened me somehow. Memories of how powerful Bastet was when a child was involved flashed through mind and I felt it fueling me more somehow.

My bossed just smiled as he watched me advance on him. He was liking the pure look of hatred in my eyes. The pure desire to destroy him with my bare hands. He got some sick pleasure out of this. He was just plain evil and I wanted to be the one to remove him from the world.

But I didn't get close enough to touch him as I was struck over the back of my head. The world went black as pain hit me harder than whatever hit me to knock me out. The only thing I remembered was calling out for my father with my heart.

~~Siris' Point Of View~~

I cupped my face in my hand. We had been at it for hours. Osiris standing before me or pacing, encouraging me to reach out with my soul to Bea wherever she was. I was looking like a fool in my study at home doing just as he said. My attempts just keep hitting a wall of some kind. I wasn't strong enough. My soul wasn't strong enough to get to Bea so I could save her.

"That's the last trick I know and I'm the god of death. Souls are my thing." I wish I could have found humor in the way he just said that, but I couldn't. Not with Bea still gone. My soul ached to just have her back and in my arms. Just to know she was alright again.

I snorted without humor before I sighed. "There's something that we're missing. Something that would help me reach Bea wherever she is being kept." It was the only explanation for our lack of results.

My head lifted when my study doors were thrown open. My heart sank again seeing Bea's father marching in. His eyes flicked to Osiris and I stood up tilting my head to the side in confusion. "I see you're here. Surely you two can find her."

Osiris frowned as he sat on the edge of my desk. "You can see me?"

President Raimon Gratton rolled his eyes before he looked right at Osiris. In another second, he wasn't the older man I had always known. Before us both stood a man who looked nearly my age and Osiris' age. A man with golden eyes and golden sun kissed skin. His pure black hair having an extremely sharp contrast where it touched his skin.

"Ra!" Osiris then groaned. "That's why it took forever when I released her soul. It had to find you and be your child."

Raimon looked puzzled. "What are you talking about?"

Osiris turned to me. "That might be the reason our attempts aren't working. Why she couldn't choose between you and my son as well."

Raimon gripped Osiris' cloak. "You're saying my daughter is the one that released Horus?!"

I stepped in. "She didn't have a choice at the time."

Raimon turned sharply away. "I will not lose another daughter because of that son of yours." Raimon looked to the sky. "Not when I just started to know her and she's forgive me for all the years we've missed together because of my own stubbornness."

Osiris stood up with his shoulders squared. "It wasn't my son's fault! Even now I fear he is stuck in his tomb unable to save your daughter. That tomb which keeps him weak and powerless. If he was free from it at the moment, he would have whisked her out of harms way by now. But she's not here with us. The one who really caused Bastet's death is behind this. You need to believe me this time."

Raimon turned on Osiris. "Bastet would still be with us if she hadn't fallen for your son."

Osiris looked at Raimon with pity. "Have you in your infinite wisdom ever noticed Bea's soul? Have you even gotten close enough to look?"

Raimon was taken aback by this turn with Osiris. "What does her soul have to do with Bastet and how she died?"

Osiris placed a hand on Raimon's shoulder. "Bea is Bastet reincarnated. I had released her soul to find the true instructor in her death and help free my son when I failed to find them myself. It took over a hundred years for her soul to find new life."

Raimon sank into one of my guest seats. "Bea is Bastet?" Raimon became the old man once again as I think that was how he felt at the moment.

Osiris knelt in front of Raimon. "Yes, but she's in need of her father's help. She only came into this life because of her love for you. Her soul couldn't bare having anyone else as her father, so it had waited. She loves you very deeply." Osiris laughed. "Her soul may have stuck near you to ensure she would be your child when you created one with a mortal."

Raimon scrubbed his face. "I thought I was still grieving over her death. How could I have known that really was her soul I saw those few times?" He closed his eyes against the pain he was feeling. What we all were feeling.

"But now she needs all our help. Siris and I have been trying to locate her but we seem to be hitting a thick wall. His soul connection with her isn't enough. I need help figuring out how to find her."

I saw Raimon squeeze his eyes just a bit tighter and after a while his brow furled. "I too can't find her." He looked at Osiris. "I see more of a pyramid than a wall over northern africa and the middle east. I have a very large area, but I can't get closer."

Osiris and I looked at each other. The same thought came to us. "Egypt." We said together. My soul instantly felt a hint closer to Bea and I knew we were right about where she was.

Raimon frowned. "You both think she was taken there?"

I nodded. "If we look in Egypt or go there, I might be able to sense her better."

But Osiris looked like he had a different thought. "I don't think it's the location that will help." He looked at me. "I believe you need my son's help."

Raising an eyebrow at him, I had only one thought. "Why?"

"You and my son each are connected to her. You both are apart of her heart and soul. She couldn't decide between you two and I think there is a reason for that."

"Together we'd be strong enough to get to her?"

Osiris smiled. "Exactly."

Raimon slammed his hands against my desk. His appearance once again turning to that of Ra. His whole body was tense as he was furious Osiris even suggested his son being tied to another. "I will not allow anyone else to release him. One of his followers killed my beloved Bastet. My daughter died because she tied herself to him."

Osiris took Raimon's collar this time. "Here me now and fully Ra. My son did no such thing. Why would he when they had tried for a child? She was killed because she had conceived. We two would have been grandfathers!"

Raimon paled. "Bastet was with child?" He slumped back into his seat. The old man appearing once more.

Osiris nodded. "The time for a soul to enter had yet been reached. It was in that time the real culprit had to act. If the child had gained a soul, Bastet would have stopped at nothing to protect it and her wrath would have overshadowed your own. Do you understand now why I had so desperately wished to be heard before you sentenced my son wrongly."

Raimon shook his head. "That wouldn't have changed the outcome. Horus could have regretted the conceiving and sought to end the tying."

Osiris sighed as he reached into cloak and withdrew a small figuring. A figurine that looked like a cat and a hawk together. "My son had created this out of the sand beside his tent when he returned to protect the Pharaoh. He was beyond happy to try again if they hadn't succeed the first time around. He wanted to be with Bastet for all eternity."

He set the figure into Raimon's hands. Osiris continued as he watched Raimon touch the figurine tenderly. "I had found it when you were carting my son away from the mortals in secret. There were even drawings of designs he was going to add to it. Gems to glitter for their child. He wanted a child with her so bad."

Raimon shook his head. "You know our laws. I can't undo what has been done. He isn't to be seen or heard from by anyone." Regret coating his words as he realized he had done wrong to another God. One that had been innocent and sentenced too hastily.

"But Bea had seen him while he was tying her to him." They both looked at me and I rolled my eyes. "You above all know that we talked about everything." I pointed to Osiris. "She said that she had remembered seeing him with his hawk head placing the tattoo on her wrist."

Osiris smiled. "Because she was excluded from the rule." He looked at Raimon. "Bastet had been in the pool of souls when you decreed no one have contact with him."

I frowned. "That brings up another point. Why does Bea remember being Bastet?"

Raimon's eyes went wide. "She does?"

Osiris nodded. "I've kept that a secret too. A god's soul is different from a mortal's. I had no idea that our memories wouldn't fade within the waters. I watched as all her memories drifted out and then they swirled back into her soul. That's why I kept her soul close to me for the longest time. I feared if the others knew, they might do something to her soul that would destroy it."

"A mortal with the knowledge of the gods would be a bit dangerous." Raimon spoke aloud. "But I see she hasn't done anything with it."

"That's because I placed a tiny spell on her memories to only show when she needed them." Osiris informed us. "But that doesn't help us now. How can we get Siris and Horus to work together to find Bea?"

We went silent for a little as each of us thought it over. There was only one thing that came to my mind. "I need to be tied to Horus."

They both looked at me. Raimon was the one who spoke. "Even if he is innocent, I can't go against my own decree. He is entombed and I won't see him freed. I can't."

"Then you won't." Osiris placed a hand on my shoulder and I sucked in a breathe as the world turned upside down for a moment. He had taken me away from my office through the god's way of traveling. I didn't know where he was taking me, but we were going to Horus so he can tie himself to me.

Chapter Thirteen

Coughing and gagging against the odd feeling that hit me when I fell to my knees the second the world righted itself. "I thought you'd warn me the next time you'd do that. We had that agreement so I wouldn't hurl afterwards."

Osiris chuckled. "I did warn you. Not my fault you didn't prepare fast enough." He turned and started walking away very proud of himself.

When I looked around rising up on unsteady legs, I was able to take in my surroundings. "Bubastis?"

"Where else would I take you when we need to get you tied to my son?"

"So we're going with my plan?"

He nodded as we came up to a deserted work station. He took a pen and started drawing on a piece of paper. "As my son is cut off from Bea, he can tie another to him temporarily. But he only knows one tying. I need you to show him this even if you can't see him."

He turned back to me. "I'm trusting you two to do this and get her back. The moment he finishes, our tying with have been cut till you two are no longer tied. That means I can't help you with anything."

Osiris turned back, but continued talking as he drew. "I'll give you instructions for what you two need to do together to find her. Only together can you locate her and save her." His hand stilled for a second. "Please save her."

"Even if it costs my life, I will."

He stopped and turned to me. "The thing is, it will cost you your life. Your death is very close. This could be the last time we're together till you come to me and the pool of souls." He looked sad in thinking I was going to died, but he knew this was going to happen eventually.

I placed my hand on his shoulder. How odd that those red eyes never affected me from moment one. They always felt comforting in their eeriness. "Then I'll die knowing my last act helped save the woman I love."

Osiris closed his eyes. "You love her more than I've seen anyone love another."

I smiled when he looked at me. "If you hadn't saved me, I wouldn't know this kind of love. It also helps that I had known I have been on borrowed time even if I wished I had more time with her."

With an unsteady hand, Osiris completed the design. "We should get to my son." I knew everything was affecting Osiris, but he was trying to be strong for us all. Because of our tie, I knew he was ready for all this to be over. He's been working to save his son for too long it feels like. I wanted to end this for him just as much as I wanted it to just b over with.

We reached the shaft that had been created after Bea fell through the collapsed floor. A rope still descended down below into the pure blackness created by how incredible far down it went. As of late, no one was to enter the chamber after the initial study of it. The government wanted to wait a little longer before we continued. Also since I was back to teaching, they wanted to hold off till I was free again. Guess that won't be happening.

Osiris handed me the design and a small box after I grabbed a lantern. "My son doesn't have anything to make a new tattoo with down there. This will help him create the new design."

I smiled lightly. "I saw what he used for Bea but didn't see the ink anywhere."

He grimaced. "He used his own blood for ink. I don't think you want that."

I shuttered. "Thanks for thinking of something else."

Osiris reached into cloak for something else. "You'll also need this." He pulled out a bottle of my whisky.

I chuckled taking it. "Raiding my good stuff?"

He frowned. "No. I just grabbed it on our way here."

Shaking my head, I stuffed the bottle down my shirt before grabbing the rope and started down the dark shaft after he told me what

Horus and I needed to do. Osiris watched me go down as the lantern dangled off my belt showing me the distance. My heart pounding because I hoped this worked. That Horus and my combined effort can get passed what cuts us off from Bea. That together, we can save her.

Finally to the bottom, I unhook the lantern and shone it around me. As I had suspected, nothing had changed much since I had left. "I don't know if you can hear me Horus, but I seriously need your help. Bea needs your help."

I spun around quickly when I heard something topple over. The light in my hand shone on a makeshift table that had somehow fallen over. I knew he had done that. Sometimes he had done something like that when I just stared at Bea as she worked. Every time I had looked at her with love and I think he had gotten jealous.

"We have a plan, but it involves you tying to me temporarily." I held up the design and then it was snatched out of my hand disappearing. "Your father drew that so you could use it. I even have a kit you can use to put it on me." I held that up and it too vanished. So he had been listening.

Next thing I knew, I was forced onto my butt and my shirt ripped right at my shoulder. I grunted and unscrewed the cap on the bottle as I felt him start shoving ink into my shoulder near my shoulder blade. I took a deep drink and felt a pause. Thankfully the alcohol kicked in when he started really tattooing me.

"You better be making it look pretty."

"Don't worry. It looks exactly as my father's design indicates."

I whipped my head around, but I still couldn't see him. "I just heard you."

A dark chuckled as I was forced to look forward again. "That is because I just finished that part of it. When I'm done, you'll be able to see me too, and touch me. Now hold still mortal."

I took another swig of whisky as he continued. Time just slipped by us as he stuck me over and over again. The ink slipping into my skin and a cloth wiping away the bits that come back out.

My eyes started to droop as I started to nod off. I humphed when he slapped my back right on the tattoo he just created. "Done scrawny mortal."

I frowned as I turned to him. "Not nice." My voice not even betraying my gawking at his very muscular self. I was even more happy to know that Bea still choose to love me too faced with this kind of god.

He shrugged. As he moved I saw that he looked pale and weak, but slowly he was looking better. "If you don't mind, I wish to get out of here."

I stood up and he did too, though I could see that he was weak. Extending my hand, he eyed it for a second before taking it. I was more than prepared for the shift in my perception when he lifted us out of the chamber.

The moment we were out of the, Horus took a deep breathe and instantly he looked like how he should be. Completely strong and unstoppable. So imposing that I doubt anyone would be foolish enough to stand up against him.

He turned to me. "Now what has happened to my beloved mortal. Why was I not allowed back with her and why did you have to be tied with me?"

I raised my chin high against his intimidating stare. "She's been taken and we can't find her. You're..." I was cut off as he raised a hand and closed his eyes.

After a few minutes, he growled and looked at me pissed off. "I cannot find her."

I rolled my eyes at him. "Of course you couldn't. If Bea's father and I couldn't doing the same thing, what would make you think you could do better."

He snarled at me. "Watch your tone boy."

A snort came out. "No can do muscles. We need to work together. Only together can we get to Bea and save her from the one who killed her before."

That made him tilt his head at me. "Before?"

I tilted my head right back at him. "You don't know this, but Bea was and is Bastet reincarnated."

Before my eyes, I saw this uber strong god just freeze. I could see in his eyes that he was trying to wrap his mind around what I just told him. Seeing everything with that bit of information. How he didn't see it before, but now it was so clear.

"There's something else."

He focused back on me. "What else could there be?" His eyes narrowed ever so much.

A grimace passed by my face. "Ra is Bea's biological father."

Horus was breathing hard. "But Ra would never hurt his child like Bea's father had."

"When we get her back, you can argue with him all you want about how crappy he's been to her."

Horus frowned at me. "But his decree will still hold. He nor anyone else that I'm not tied to will ever see, hear, or touch me."

I scrubbed my face. "I forgot for a second." With a heavy sigh, I sat down indian style. "And after this is over with, I won't be able to because I'll be dead."

He mirrored my posture as he scowled in confusion. "You seem very calm knowing this."

I shrugged pulling out my swiss army knife. "I've known for a while and was just happy that I got to love a wonderful woman." My hand with the knife rested in my lap. "I will confess that I wanted to love her longer. For years. And I had wanted to see the child she carries be born before I died."

Shaking my head before a tear fell, I put the knife to my palm and made a small cut. The new pain I created couldn't mask the one I was feeling knowing my death was so close. "We need to have our blood mingle together as we both reach out with our souls to Bea. We each have formed a connection with her. Our combined connection should be strong enough to pierce the barrier keeping us from her."

Horus pulled out a small dagger from a strap on his ankle. The blade had hieroglyphics that shone with an eerie gleam in the light. He placed it in his palm and did as I had done. His skin failing to resist against his blade.

Placing our palms together, we both closed our eyes and I felt a surge go through my soul. I could feel him with me as I knew I was with him. Together we were reaching out for Bea. Together we both desperately wanted Bea back and safe. To love her as we couldn't help doing.

We came to the barrier and hit it for a moment. I could feel him shove at it. When he reared his hand back, I did the same wanting to help him get through so we both could get to Bea. I knew we both needed to break passed it.

And together we had. The instant our combined strike hit, we were thrusted through and we both stumbled in our soul form to the concrete floor. Even in this form, I could feel what everything felt like.

Next came dizziness as Horus pulled our physical forms to us and I felt sick to my stomach having been brought back into my body before I knew what was going to happen. I rushed over to a corner and puked. He was chuckling because he had done that on purpose and was delighted that I was sick because of it.

"Shall we search for her?" His voice laced with dark humor.

I stood up and wiped my mouth closing my eyes. "I feel her. She's close."

"That I feel her too. She's unconscious." He walked passed me. "This way."

We rounded a corner and we both stopped next to each other. But we weren't the only ones in this new hallway, four guys dressed in black clothes snapped their heads to me. A small curse slipped out as they started to charge at me.

"Guess I have to deal with these bastards by myself."

"Not all by yourself."

Horus stepped in front of me and as the first guy reached us with a riot baton raised, he threw out his left hand and gripped the guy's baton thrusting it toward the guy's face. It connected with the guy's nose forcing the guy backwards. The man's face was priceless along with his buddies.

I smirked as they looked at me. "Yeah, I'm not alone."

Horus pulled out a strip of cloth and bound his hand like a boxer. A smirk on his face as hieroglyphics shimmered in the torch light that dotted the walls. "I may not be able to touch them normally, but this will help them feel my hits.

I shook my head as I looked to see that my words just seemed to piss them off. "For our God!!!"

They had a battle cry? These guys are psycho! Horus took care of two and I took care of the other two. No one was about to stop us rescuing our beloved. Horus seemed to be more furious now that he knew who Bea was in a previous life.

In moments, we had them all out cold. I dusted off my hands as we started again toward where we both felt Bea was. Odd how my connection to Horus was far different from the connection I had with Osiris than I thought it was going to be.

"I find it odd too."

I stopped Horus. "What do you mean? Where you just reading my mind?"

He frowned. "I thought you just spoke aloud." His brows scrunched together. "I've never heard of this kind of connection let alone with someone I'm not permanently tied to."

I shook myself. "We can't puzzle over this."

He nodded sharply. "You're right. Later."

"You can say that." I shoved passed him. "I won't be alive later."

Chapter Fourteen

~~Bea's Point Of View~~

A slap brought me back to reality. Not a light slap either. My cheek burned and my eyes watered from the slap. My head and my cheek both throbbed in tandem with each other. Neither having more presence than the other.

A hand brutally gripped my chin and I was forced to look at my old boss. He tsked at me like a imprudent child. "Now look what you had one of my followers and I do to you. Guess I should have expected something like that. You're more god than any mortal could ever be, though you've never known your whole life." He chuckled. "Not just your soul is god, but one of your parents was as well."

He tilted his head to the side as if he was thinking leisurely. "I doubt it's your mother as she died. No that can't be the parent that you get your god side from. No, it has to be your father. That bastard that left you in my hands all those years ago."

I spat in his face. Feeling satisfied as he had to close his eye or it would have flown right into it. "You lied to him about me. You took so many years away from us."

He wiped my spit off his face. "How else was I to keep you under my control? Let you just go away? I think not. Now that I know that your father is a god, I'm doubly glad that I managed to turn him against you."

I thrashed under him feeling that he was stretched completely across me. "Get off ME!"

He just laughed at my meek attempts trying to get free from under him. I didn't care that both my wrists and ankles were bound tightly with other metal shackles. Or that they started to burn under my attempts. All I wanted was for him to get away from me. He ruined my life for so many years and now he's trying to do it again. Permanently this time.

He just laughed. "Not this time." He smirked down at me. "These new shackles have been spelled to bind your god half. You're pure mortal right now." He grinned darkly and my stomach twisted sickly. "As I prefer you."

I glared at him. "You will regret this." My threat, though may have been hollow, was powerful.

He just kept smirking as if it were nothing at all. "And who will stop me?"

"US!" My heart did a strange and happy flip at the sound of Siris' voice. My old boss Seth was flown to the other side of the room as Siris appeared next to me. His hands going right to the shackle that bound my right wrist. He tugged and tried to quickly pry it open, but it just wouldn't budge.

"Ha!" Seth rose from where he hit the concrete wall as if unharmed, even though he hit the wall harder than I thought any mortal could survive. I doubt he was at all mortal or harmed. "You can't remove my shackles. Only I have the key to them."

I saw Siris snap his head up to the other side of the bed I was stretched across. He frowned. "You can't think of that now. So what if he had pulled Osiris apart once, Bea needs us to unbind her. We need to get her out of here. You can get vengeance for that later when she's free and safe."

Giving Siris a strange looked, he gave me a forced lopsided smile before showing me his shoulder that had a brand on it. In the center was Horus' symbol. "I got your god with me so we could get to you."

Seth growled. "Horus is here?!"

Siris smirked at Seth darkly. "That's right. Together we're strong enough to break your barrier." He stood up. "And if you don't want us to kill you, hand over the key." He smiled more. "There's another that would like so much to get their hands on you."

"And who would that be?"

Siris shrugged as he walked over to Seth. "Ra." He said it so casually as if he said that every day of his life.

The walls shook and I felt heat wash over me for a second. Siris looked over to the other side of the bed as my left shackle felt like it was moving now from someone, Horus, attempting to unbind me. "Guess the old man heard me." There was a joke there that I just didn't get.

Seth snarled as he lunged forward and Siris stiffened. I screamed as my eyes took in the bloody hand that held a pumping heart. Siris' heart. Seth had gone right through Siris' body and grabbed his heart. His still beating heat.

With a push, Siris' body fell to the ground and he was quickly dying. Seth loomed over while Siris' eyes clouded. "You're a fool for being so close to a god and thinking you had something over them. No one else will enter this place and save her. You failed."

"NOOOO!!!" My soul screamed out as I watched Siris' body go limp. His life leaving just an empty shell on the floor. A hole forming in my heart as one of my guys was taken from me forever.

~~Siris' Point Of View~~

Bea's scream echoed in my head as I was pulled away from my body. I had failed. Saving Bea was all that had mattered, and I didn't even get her out of the shackles. Horus must be entombed again because of my blunder. My arrogance that led to our down fall.

I was slammed down on a hard surface and was shocked when a second grunt came from next to me. The fog that was in front of my eyes was too thick to see anything in front of my eyes. The other person must have the same problem as I heard him searching around, feeling around for a second.

"Rise both of you." A voice I didn't recognize drifted through the fog and seemed to be more than one voice. An odd feeling was carried with the voice that I just couldn't place.

Lifting up, I found that it was Horus with me. We looked at each other puzzled. "You're not back in your tomb."

He raised an eyebrow. "And you just died."

"Correction, he would be dead in one more heartbeat if we had not stopped time and brought you both here." We both turned sharply to the feminine voice that shifted to a male voice towards the end of their sentence.

"Shai. What is going on?" Horus stared even more puzzled at the figure that stood several feet away from both of us.

The male figure before us shifted to a female form. Both had pure black hair and long slender frames. The female smiled at us. "Fate dear boys. One we have kept to ourselves till now knowing how the events had to play out."

The male figure walked over to Horus. "We could not come to your defense knowing *he* would have gotten away permanently even if we had. You needed time before revenge could be sought."

The figure became a female and turned to me. "And you needed to be tied to him before what we are about to do could happen." She walked over to me and placed her hand over my heart. "Will you do anything to save the woman you love?"

"Take my soul and destroy it if that saves her." Nothing mattered but Bea. My beloved mortal goddess.

The male turned to Horus. "What of you?"

Horus rose his chin in the air. "Take my immortality and soul, and destroy them if it meant that my beloved lives and is safe."

The figure smiled at us shifting easily between male and female. "Then what has been two shall become one. Both born anew and unique. Both crafted for the one they love."

I gasped as something shot through me. There was an identical gasped from Horus as the same thing happened to him. I felt it as if we were experiencing this together. Just like after we were tied together. Everything went black and white at the same time.

Let this save Bea...

~~Bea's Point Of View~~

My tears fell as I turned my head away from the sight of Siris' body. I couldn't see his body lying there dead. A part of me ached for it not to be real. I didn't want him to die because of me.

Seth just walked over to a water basin and washed his hand and arm as if it were nothing to kill someone like that. He smirked at me as he looked over his shoulder. "Now you know that I'm a God, aren't you turned on?"

I shook my head. "You're a monster!" The feeling of being sick rose up.

He laughed. "No, I just love causing chaos." Wiping his hands, he tossed the cloth to the side and came over to the bed I laid upon. "Now that I'm free to do as I please, let's remove that nasty symbol of Horus' and replace it with mine so no other will ever have you."

The door opened and a servant came in with a cattle brand that was red hot. The man glanced down at Siris' body and then snapped his head away. He seemed a bit shaky seeing a dead body on the floor.

Seth took the poker from the man not needing the gloves the man had to use so he didn't burn himself. The man bowed his head before he came over to me. In a very swift movement, he had the band stripped off my wrist and flung across the room. He held my arm still as I struggled in his hold. Seth smiled as he came over with the poker. The symbol for Set was what glowed a threatening red.

"Now hold still my little mortal. This will only hurt for a moment till you pass out from the pain." Seth seemed to revel in that thought.

"You will do no such thing." I stopped struggling as the other froze too at the sound of that voice.

We all turned to where Siris' body laid, and I sucked in a lung full of air. He wasn't dead. His body rose and where there had been a hole that Seth created was now closed as if nothing had happened. The only evidence that he had been struck through the heart by Seth was the blood that stuck his shirt to his back around a hole in the material.

With a simple flick of his hand, the shirt came cleanly away from Siris' body. As his muscles flexed, they seemed to grew a bit more. They became full and reminded me of the ones upon Horus' body. How uber strong Horus always looked and was.

Seth growled as he thrusted the poker back to his servant who scrambled to get hold of it without burning himself. A feat I was shocked that he managed to complete. "I'll kill you again!" Seth threatened as he advanced.

But Siris paid him no mind. He just sighed and took a huge breathe of the life given back to him. "I think not." He said as if to just say something out loud to himself. A simple soft breathe from part of that breathe of life he took in a half a moment ago.

I held my breathe the moment Seth was in reaching distance to Siris. Fear that Seth was about to end Siis' new life just when it began again. But Seth didn't get the chance to do anything. Siris spun around and gripped Seth by the throat tightly. Siris grinned so darkly as he stared Seth down. "Hello Set. You have much to pay for."

Seth flew like a ragged doll into the thick concrete wall causing a huge crater in it. Seth wobbled as he came out being phased for the first time since I've known him. He gawked at Siris who just cracked most of his bones as his muscles have indeed had grown bigger the more time that has passed.

"How did you? No mortal has ever thrown me like a God can." Seth had been shaken at this new development. His voice no longer carried the strength of a God he claimed to be.

Siris just continued to flex his body out. "That is because I'm no longer a mortal." He grinned. "Say hello to the new me." He advanced over to Seth. "Shai has recreated me into what I am now. Siris has been combined with Horus to create me." He dragged Seth to him by his neck. "And you have pissed off the wrong man who loves that woman twice over."

Siris reached down and Seth screamed loudly as I turned away when I noticed what Siris had done. He had ripped Seth's testicles right off of him. "That was for Osiris." He just tossed Seth aside and turned to me. "As for what you've done to my beloved and were going to do, I'll let Ra take over your punishment."

As Siris came over to me, the servant dropped the poker and rushed over to Seth. Too bad the servant wasn't really thinking or he would have known how foolish that move was on his part. Seth snapped his neck when he went to try and help his God.

Before I could blink, Siris had the chains snapped and I was lifted into his arms. The collar gone from my neck as well in the next moment.

My eyes stayed in his that looked down at me. "You might want to hold tight. We're about make a quick exit."

I nodded as I wrapped my arms around his neck. My forehead pressing into the side of his neck as he tightened his arms just a little more around me and I felt love wrap around me. A love even bigger than what I felt with Siris or Horus separately. As if it was both of them that held me and protected me. As if they were one in the same now and their combined love for me was so much more.

A deep chuckled sounded and I looked up at him. He smiled down at me as he brought up a soft caress of his fingers along my sore cheek. "Let me fix this." As his fingers moved, the pain lifted from not just my cheek, but everywhere that had hurt.

When everything felt better, I opened my eyes that had closed with his touch. I just couldn't help myself. Lifting up, I kissed him soundly. He smiled as he took over the kiss.

We pulled apart swiftly when someone cleared their throat. I blushed seeing my father. "You both can get back to that in a moment." He walked over to us and Siris set me down on my feet. My father pulled my to him and held me. "Are you alright?"

I nodded as I crumbled into him. "Thank you dad." My dad nodded and held me up. His ams tightening just a bit as a few tears landed on his shirt.

My father then looked at Siris and his eyes narrowed. "You're fused together."

I looked at Siris and he smiled at me. Then he shook his head and I saw Horus' hawk head, but it was different. The eyes stayed human and the feathers seemed longer in the back at the top. So much longer that they curved downward some.

Before I knew what I was doing, I was walking up to him and stroked the feathers along his cheek. He closed his eyes, but then snapped them open as I felt very weak. My hand falling and hitting his shoulder. My body following soon after.

He caught me shaking his head back to normal. My father placing his hand on Siris' shoulder as my eyes started to close. "I don't think you need to worry. What has happened just caught up to her. I'll go deal with the one responsible."

"I made sure to have placed his compound with a closing barrier. No one in and no one out so you have the honor of dealing out more punishment. His own has been destroyed so you may enter at your leisure."

"And the one responsible will suffer dearly." I felt warmth caress my face before I slipped the rest of the way asleep. I was safe and in my love's arms. No better place to be in all the world.

Chapter Fifteen

I smiled as I felt feather kisses along the edge of my shoulder. "Morning my love." I opened my eyes and glanced across to Siris as he laid next to me. He smiled and I smiled back.

"Morning."

His hand graced my hair as he leaned down. With such gentleness, his lips adored mine. I too adored him loving how he had saved me. How he felt different yet complete as he moved me to my back. Willingly and openly I let our passion grow till the point where we had to be one. He made love to me and it took me to a new high. I felt his love through every touch and every thrust.

Afterwards, I trembled for some time because of his added skill. He just hovered over me and stared at my belly. "I had feared I'd never see this little baby grow within you and be born." He looked at me and I saw a tear fall. "When I was dying, all I regretted was that I wasn't going to get to see how beautiful you would be throughout your whole pregnancy and on our wedding day if you still want to marry me."

My eyes softened. "Of course I will always want to marry you. Things were so complicated before that I was confused. I'm not confused anymore."

He smiled as he reached over to the bedside table. Now noticing that we were in his room. On his bedside table was a small velvet box that made my breathe catch. "I've had this for a month now. I just couldn't help getting it when I saw it. I was holding onto it for the right time." He looked up at me after he opened the small box. "Will you wear it knowing it is the symbol of my love for you and I want forever with you?"

My eyes fluttered down to the delicate ring in the small box and felt myself melt more into him. "How could I not?" He chuckled as he took the ring out and slipped it on my finger with a kiss.

As I looked at him, what Seth had said about my father came back to me. "My father's a God, isn't he?"

Siris rested his chin just below my sternum. "Yes he is, but he should be the one to reveal whom he is." I nodded and he slipped the rest of the way up my body. "How did you find out?"

"Seth told me I was half God. Since my mother had died, he concluded it was my father."

He dragged his soft silky finger tips down along my cheekbone. "He didn't hurt you, did he?"

I gave Siris a small smile. "You had fixed what he had done to me." I looked at my wrist. "He was going to take it away from me."

Siris leaned over and kissed my tattoo. It tingled and when he pulled away, it changed. No longer was there the tying symbols or the fully defined symbol of Horus. It looked beautiful with soft yet vibrant colors. Filigree lit on either side of the faint symbol that made the tattoo look more artistic than anything else.

"We need not be tied together like that any longer. But I thought you'd like to have something to remember how fate brought us back together." He looked at me. "My blessed Bastet that many including myself still love beyond all the Gods."

I smiled at him then blushed as my stomach growled deeply. Siris laughed as he hopped up from the bed to grab what was laying across the cushioned bench at the foot of his bed. All I did was blink and then I was up and the wrap dress was on me.

I pouted. "Having fun."

He gave me a look of innocence. "Half of me is finding new ways to experience being a God."

A giggle came out. "This will be something I need to get used too. One mighty man instead of one God and one man."

He smiled as he pulled me to his now t-shirt and jeans clad self. "I can show you all you can do too now that you know you're half God."

I looked down at his chest where my fingers lazily made circles. "But I might not be able to do all you can."

He lifted my chin and kissed me. "If I can, you can. We are equal in our God-ness." He bent down and lifted me up into his arms. "I think Shai knew and planned this the whole time."

My lip pouted was he walked without pause down the back stairs. "But yours is more than mine."

He shook his head as he sat me down on the breakfast nook bench. Leaning down, he smiled. "Don't be too sure about that. You're father is very powerful and I know for a fact that you're strong too."

"How?"

He leaned down more causing me to lean back against the back of the bench. "I saw those shackles. The metal had bent under your struggles and that's before you had been trained to harness what is inside you."

"Ah-hem." We turned to see Jilliann holding a tray. "If you don't mind sir, sit."

Siris chuckled as he took his seat next to me. Unlike all the other times when we were sort of hiding our affection, he took my hand fully on the table. Jilliann smiled as she set the tray down and placed a bowl of cream of wheat in front of me. Siris got an overflowing plate of eggs, potato hash, and meat. My nose scrunching at the smell that hit me.

"And that's why I knew to give you a more simple breakfast." She smiled as she placed small dishes with topping in front of me. "Just wait till the real morning sickness hits you. You'll be thanking me for keeping your breakfasts simple and easy on you."

She leaned down and kissed my cheek. "I'm glad they were able to get you back to us." She smiled at the hand Siris held. "And I'm delighted you two aren't keeping that bit a secret." I blushed as she turned away.

Siris lifted my hand and kissed the inside of my wrist. "I don't want to keep us a secret any longer." He looked at me with those deep eyes of his. "I want to shout to the heavens with how much I'm in love with you."

My blush grew more. "As I love you."

He leaned over and kissed me softly. "That I have had no doubt about ever."

I whimpered when my stomach growled again and he just chuckled pulling away. "I'll let you eat now." He placed his hand over my belly again. "You're not eating just for one anymore." He smiled up at me. "I find that very sexy."

"Okay okay, down boy. Let's eat."

He chuckled as we started eating. After I went through my bowl of hot cereal, I rose and went to Jilliann pouting. She laughed and made me something else to eat. She said it was a good thing I had an appetite at the moment. She even made me a delicious potato hash with a little bit of fish pieces as I was slightly craving fish.

After breakfast, Siris insisted that I relax as much as I could today. He wanted me to just forget about what happened to me because it didn't matter right now. That however was squashed when detectives came to talk to me about what happened. Siris wasn't happy about it at all.

"Please, is this necessary right now? Can't you come back tomorrow. I don't want her stressed as she's in a very delicate condition."

I placed my hand on Siris' arm before I turned to the detectives. "You must understand that the last time I was stressed resulted me being in the hospital and then I was taken the moment I was released."

The detective closest to me nodded. "We fully understand and we'll be as soft about this as we can. If at any point you're getting too stress, we'll stop for now and come back when you feel better."

Nodding, Siris took my hand as the detectives started to ask me questions about what happened. Apparently they were told that my father had hired a special agency to find and rescue me. It was the best explanation about how I was saved so quickly.

I started to feel sick, and Siris said that it was enough for now. The detectives said that they had only a few more questions, but they could wait till I was feeling better. After the detectives were seen out, Siris coaxed me to lay down along the couch as he knelt on the floor next to me.

He moved my hair away from my forehead. "Do you feel a little better?"

I nodded as I placed the back of my hand on my forehead. "This does help."

"How about this?" He placed his hands on my belly and chest.

Warmth spread through me and I smiled. "You healing me?"

"No healing, but helping. Because you tapped into your God half, healing you is a bit harder to do." I looked at him and he smiled. "You never tapped into it before because you didn't know you had that kind of side. Now you do, and I'll help you know more of it. I'll teach all you want to know." He leaned down and kissed me. "For now, just relax. I'll be your devoted servant for you to command." He moved to hover over me with a smug and playful smile. "Tell me your first command." He leaned down and grazed his lips against my ear. "Command me."

I arched my back a little as I gripped his upper arms because his soft words had spark desire. "Make love to me again." I was breathless with want.

He chuckled and slipped his head farther down placing feather light kisses along the length of my neck. "Your wish is my command."

"Sorry kiddies, but you have company."

We groaned as Siris got off of me. When I sat up, I noticed my father wearing something other than a business suit for once. I tried to see if I could figure out which God he was, but I just couldn't place which one he was. He didn't seem like any God I'd think of right off the top of my head.

My father smiled down at me as he came over and crouched in front of the couch. He took my hands and gave me a little squeeze. "I've taken care of that now-unable-to father-children sorry excuse for a God." I pouted and he smiled. "Set is going to rue the day he even started his obsession with my daughter and making me turn away from you."

I smiled at my dad. "I was told that you tried to find me and come save me."

He hung his head down a little. "Set had placed my name along with others within the barrier spell to keep us from finding you. I wanted so desperately to do right by you after I did so wrong for so long."

I wrapped my arms around his neck and hugged him. He hugged me back and it felt like he was relieved. "Thank you."

My dad pulled back and looked over to where Siris was leisurely sitting down on the other end of the couch. "I'm stealing her away from you for a good bit of today." He looked to me with a bit of nervousness. "If you will spend time with me."

I looked over at Siris and he smiled shrugged. "As long as she relaxes and isn't stressed by anything today." He pouted. "I had wanted to just have a lay around day with my fiancee."

My father's eyebrows shot up and when he turned to me, I showed him the ring Siris gave me. He smiled and hugged me tightly again. "He's made it official!" I nodded as I felt myself tearing up. My father pulled me to him stroking my hair. I felt like a little girl being coddled for the first time by a real father.

"Is she alright?"

My dad nodded. "I think she's just weepy right now. With everything that happened, I think she's still needing time to come to terms with it."

Sniffling, I pulled back. My dad had a handkerchief out and helped wipe my tears away. "Sorry." I hated crying in front of others, especially now when it could happen randomly.

He shook his head wiping the last tear away. "Nothing at all to be sorry for. Just take a deep breathe." I did. "Better?" I nodded because I did feel better.

I looked to Siris. "Is it okay if I spent time with my dad?"

He leaned down and kissed my cheek. "Anything that makes you happy." Pulling back, he had a smile on his face. "And that will give me a chance to plan a romantic date for us later tonight."

I frowned and he laughed with my dad. Siris looked at me as if I shouldn't be frowning. "We are going on a date tonight and you're going to buy a very beautiful dress for it with your father's help."

~~~

My father turned around and held another dress up. The twenty millionth one and I was getting a bit tired of dress shopping. Yet here was my own flesh and blood father looking happy to try and help me with finding the perfect dress. I would have been fine with anyone he choose already, but he insists there was always one better.
~~~

I sat on the cushioned couch and frowned. "That is too revealing for me. I'd look like an over paid hooker for my date."

He turned the dress around and looked at it. Shaking his head, he handed it to the sales lady that was helping us. She took it as she too looked at it and shook her head now seeing what I saw.

My father sighed sitting next to me as the sales lady went to get more dresses. I shifted again in my seat. For the past two shops he's taken me into, I've felt a slight cramp along the sides of my abs.

He placed a hand on my arm. "Are you alright?" When I looked up at him, he had a look of worry. "You need a break." He shook his head. "I've been dragging you around to all these shops and haven't thought of a break for you."

Smiling at him, I placed my hand over his. "I'm fine." I shifted again. "Just feeling a bit uncomfortable at the moment."

He rose and tug on my hand. "Then you need a break from this." He turned to the sales lady to tell her that we will return after I had a moment to breath from the shopping.

It was when she nodded that a lady behind me gasped after I stood up. I turned to see what happened when my eyes caught sight of a red spot upon the couch I was just sitting on in the place I sat. Looking down to the floor beneath me and saw three drops of blood fall. The blood was from me. My hands went to my belly as my thoughts went to my baby. My legs giving out under my fear for the life of my child.

My dad caught me. "Just think about the baby and hold it tight in your heart and mind. The baby will be alright. Just know it will be." He held me as sales ladies started rushing around and calling for an ambulance. My father just kept chanting to me and rocked me as I did as he told me. My eyes closed as I willed my baby to be alright.

In no time at all, the medics arrived with a gurney. By that time, the pain had increased from a crap to excruciating tightness of the area next to my womb. I just held tight praying my baby was alright. All my hope and prayers were for my child. My father had to answer any questions the medics had as I wasn't responding to them. The only things I said to them was to beg them to help me save my baby.

At the hospital, my father was forced away when I was taken to an ER room. But I didn't think he'd have left me for long. I felt a hand in mine and looked up to see the smiling face of Ra and in that moment I knew that's who my father was. It made sense as he had been her father too. My other life, Bastet's life.

The doctor's gave me something that made me sleep. They said it was to ease my discomfort as they had to check "down there" for what is wrong. They didn't want me to be uncomfortable during the procedure.

Thinking back to the day Siris had proposed to me, I realized my father had helped me save my beautiful baby girl that was inside me. I hadn't known it then, but my father was telling me that my faith and desire to keep my baby was what saved her. That a God's mind can truly do things that would have been viewed as a miracle. We shape reality with just a thought. Even being half God, I still had that kind of ability.

Now as I watch smiling brightly while my wonderful husband was being pulled around as if he were nothing by our daughter, I am more thankful of my God side and all the things I've learned about myself. Siris has been an amazing teacher to me about that side of who I was. He's also become such an amazing father.

My father tried to teach me about my God half, but as he couldn't think like a mortal, or half mortal for that matter, when explaining about being a God, Siris had to take over. My father meant well, but there were somethings he still didn't understand about mortals. I was more than thankful when Siris took over because he understood how I thought better than anyone in all the world. Learning from him felt effortless and very pleasing.

Osiris was given special permission now to come to the mortal world without needing to tie himself to a soon to be departed mortal giving the mortal more time to live their life before a final death. It's the least my father could do for not listening to Osiris in the first place all those centuries ago. Now Osiris could come and go in the mortal world only during certain times and for a certain amount of time. My father couldn't let Osiris stay like he does as Osiris had duties in the underworld.

Siris and I tended to plan any special events around when his father could come back to the mortal world. Our wedding for one. I couldn't believe how weepy Osiris was when we said our vows. It was kind of strange seeing him as he really was though the normal mortals couldn't. His red eyes even redder from emotion.

The whole wedding had been so perfect. My father had insisted on having it at the school. He even had a wedding planner booked. Anything and everything to make up from the years we lost together. He even did the none-father-of-the-bride thing and was there with me through all the planning. He helped pick out colors with me and flowers. Imagine, Ra, God of the sun and ruler over all the Egyptian Gods doing something so mortal.

I smiled every time I think back to that day and the friendship that just grew more after that. Cilla wasn't just one of Siris' students, but was now my best friend. She even was my maid-of-honor as I couldn't think of anyone else I wanted to stand next to me.

And when I went into labor, Osiris was already there with us enjoying some family time with both of us. As he only has about three days each month, we were happy it was the first day he arrived that my water broke. He was there through it all along with my own father. Cilla unfortunately had to wait in the family room because she wasn't allowed to be in the room with me.

When I gave birth to our sweet and beautiful baby girl, almost all Siris' students came to congratulate us and see our baby. Cilla being the first one with a tiny little plushy unicorn that was pink in her arms as a birthday present. My baby girl loved the world out of that plushy till it broke in two between her hands. Cilla had pouted and when she came over next, she had a golden unicorn for our little goddess to play with.

When our daughter's birthday comes around, Osiris is there for the party. He loves doting on our daughter too just as my father loves to whenever he's allowed. Siris and I have had to rein our fathers in some times as they love to go over board.

It was when our daughter was born that I found out that Horus had been the one to give me my daughter. Her jet black hair and Horus' golden eyes were the tell for who was her father. That meant she was three quarters God where I was just half. But none of that mattered, she was my baby girl.

I looked down at my new baby bump and smiled. There was no way I could help from wanting to be pregnant again. After how complicated my first pregnancy had been, I had wanted to experience one without the stress or the pain the first one had. And I just wanted to create another life with my beloved husband.

Once Siris had arrived at the hospital, he made sure that I couldn't and didn't lift a finger for anything. I had to pout which lead to me crying when I wanted to go to his office to get some work done. He had refused for me to leave the mansion till I managed to calm down. After he got me calmed, he lifted me up and we went to his office on campus.

My father had seen that I didn't do much when I was there while Siris had his classes. There had been a rumor that my father had taken an interest in me. A romantic one, till one of Siris' students had asked me. I just laughed and told her the truth. Her jaw dropped and then she laughed as she saw the resemblance.

Funny how five years could go by so fast when I had a real family for once in my life. I didn't mind the lack of worry or wanting for anything. I had all that mattered and they were having fun in the park tumbling around while I watched on.

I even had a relationship with my father's ex-wife who had tried to open my father's eyes the time he turned away from me. It was sad finding out that was the reason their marriage had ended. But she said that she had been glad that I had my father now after all this time.

At the wedding, it seemed like my father and his ex-wife were reconnecting. My father may not understand mortals very well, but he seemed taken by his ex-wife again. They may still only be friends, but I did notice they were getting close to maybe a reconciliation. They both don't think they could do the whole marriage together again, but they could still be together.

What was taken from all of us so very long ago was ours once again, and I couldn't feel any more blessed. And even happier knowing everything was behind us. I was happy to enjoy life and my family that was all around me.